Love Shouldn't Hurt

Lock Down Publications and Ca$h
Presents

Love Shouldn't Hurt

A Novel by *Meesha*

Lock Down Publications

P.O. Box 870494
Mesquite, Tx 75187

Visit our website @
www.lockdownpublications.com

Copyright 2018 by Love Shouldn't Hurt

First Edition August 2018
Printed in the United States of America

This is a work of fiction. Names, characters, places, and incidents either are products of the author's imagination or are used fictitiously. Any similarity to actual events or locales or persons, living or dead, is entirely coincidental.

Lock Down Publications
Like our page on Facebook: Lock Down Publications @
www.facebook.com/lockdownpublications.ldp
Cover design and layout by: **Dynasty Cover Me**
Book interior design by: **Shawn Walker**
Edited by: **Tisha Andrews**

Stay Connected with Us!

Text **LOCKDOWN** to 22828 to stay up-to-date with new releases, sneak peaks, contests and more…
Or **CLICK HERE** to sign up.
Thank you.

Like our page on Facebook:

Lock Down Publications: Facebook

Join **Lock Down Publications/The New Era Reading Group**

Visit our website @ www.lockdownpublications.com

Follow us on Instagram:

Lock Down Publications: Instagram

Email Us: We want to hear from you!

Submission Guideline.

Submit the first three chapters of your completed manuscript to ldpsubmissions@gmail.com, subject line: Your book's title. The manuscript must be in a .doc file and sent as an attachment. Document should be in Times New Roman, double spaced and in size 12 font. Also, provide your synopsis and full contact information. If sending multiple submissions, they must each be in a separate email.

Have a story but no way to send it electronically? You can still submit to LDP/Ca$h Presents. Send in the first three chapters, written or typed, of your completed manuscript to:

LDP: Submissions Dept
Po Box 870494
Mesquite, Tx 75187

DO NOT send original manuscript. Must be a duplicate.

Provide your synopsis and a cover letter containing your full contact information.

Thanks for considering LDP and Ca$h Presents.

Acknowledgements

We got another one, Ladybug! I know you are up there cheering me on with every word that I type. There isn't a second that goes by that you aren't on my mind but know you are forever in my heart. Keep shining brightly, my love. This book is dedicated to my readers! Meesha's Book Soldiers are amazing! The love that has been shown for me since my first release has only grown stronger. Thank you all for giving me a chance as a new author. Majority of y'all been rocking with me from day one, but I have a relationship with all of you just the same. I'm going to try my hardest to keep the fire burning in my pen, but I don't think I have a choice because #ISSALDPTHANGBABY. LOL. Seriously, thank y'all from the bottom of my heart for rockin' with ya girl.

I want to give a special shout out to my mama! Man, without you I would be nothing. When I was going through my crap, you kept me lifted telling me that giving up was not an option. And I appreciated that so much. Then my happiness went from sugar to shit fast, my computer went down and that was my only means to keep my sanity. I didn't know what I would do, but you came to the rescue and got me another computer! You are the real MVP and I love you to the moon and back.

Happy birthday, Sandra Atueyi!

MEESHA

Chapter 1
Summer of 2011
Kaymee

Graduating high school was something that I had been waiting for all my life. It was the final step to getting from under my mama's roof. I grew up in the Cabrini Green projects on the northwest side of Chicago. I was the only child to Dorothy Morrison, but everyone called her Dot.

Dot was thirty-five but the way she acted, you'd think she was younger. She partied harder than most of the women that were in their twenties. She lived her life as if she didn't have a child to care for. In fact, I was the last person on her things to worry about list.

You would think being an only child would be a dream come true. Nope, it was hell for me. I couldn't recall when I started to notice the way Dot treated me, but I do know when it got worse. I couldn't tell anyone what a mother's love felt like because I had never experienced it.

I remembered all the nights that I had stayed home alone because she was out having fun. She didn't know what was going on in her house and obviously, she didn't care. It was a good thing that I wasn't the type of child that wanted to know what it was like to be out in the streets.

Dot cared more about alcohol and the men that came and went in her life than she cared about me. She called all of them niggas by name but called me bitch. They could lay up in our two-bedroom apartment without paying a dime but dished out plenty of dick and got mad respect in return. Me, on the other hand, had to pay three hundred dollars a month even though she only paid a hundred-fifty for rent. And I got her ass to kiss for my contributions.

I was the one that kept our apartment clean because she was always too busy entertaining stray dudes to care if it was clean or not. If I didn't keep things tidy, our place would look like many of the other apartments in this neighborhood. Dirty with lots of unwanted pets that I wasn't fond of.

Cooking was something I learned to do on my own at the age of six. It was either learn to fend for myself or starve and I wasn't about to go without eating. One thing I could say was, there was always food in the house. She had to buy groceries since she cooked all her dudes something to eat when they rolled through.

At times, I felt like I was the mother of the household. I paid the bills and didn't get any respect around that muthafucka. Not to mention how she demanded things of me like she was my evil stepmom instead of the woman that birthed me.

The things that came out of Dot's mouth when she referred to me made all types of thoughts run through my head. If I didn't have a copy of my birth certificate stating who my mother was, I would have sworn I was adopted. But unfortunately, I wasn't.

It was twelve o'clock in the afternoon when I turned over to look at the time on my phone. I stretched my body like a feline, popping every joint from my neck to my toes. The sound of slippers dragging across the floor could be heard in the hall. "Let the bullshit begin," I said to myself.

My door opened without warning, slamming into the wall. The impact of the knob banging into the wall caused a golf-sized dent. Standing in the doorway with a barely there nightgown on was none other than my mammy. The rims of her eyes were still red from all the partying she'd done the night before with her friends. So, I knew she was in rare form.

"Get the fuck up, bitch! I told you two weeks ago that you would not be in here sleeping all damn day. Don't you have to work today?" she asked nastily.

I stared at her and didn't say a word. If I were to say something, it wouldn't be anything nice. I wasn't the same kid that she would hit, pinch, punch, or push down, back in the day. I was trying not to be the woman that whooped her ass for old and new. Even though she didn't have an ounce of respect for me, I respected her because she was still my mama.

"I know yo' ass hear me talking to you. Now answer me when I ask you a question, bitch!"

"I don't have to work today. I have the next two days off," I replied, while pulling the covers up to my shoulders.

Every day she came in my room to start an argument with me. It never failed. She had a reason behind every rant, too. I wondered what she was up to on this day, but I'm sure I didn't have long to find out.

"You ain't gotta go to work, but you got to get the hell out of here. You won't be laid up in here all muthafuckin' day, so get the fuck up and find something to do with yo' life."

Chuckling to myself, I threw the covers back and swung my legs out of the bed. I shook my head back and forth with my bottom lip between my teeth. I was fighting the urge to curse her out, but I had to remember she was my mother.

"Say what the fuck you gotta say, bitch. I dare you to say something disrespectful so you can give me a reason to kick your ass," she said through clenched teeth.

I released my bottom lip from my teeth and looked her in the face. It took me a few seconds to get my thoughts together as well as calmed myself down. There were so many things that I wanted to ask but I didn't want a confrontation with her. I decided to ask a simple question to see how she would react.

"Why do you hate me so much?" I asked.

"Don't question me about shit, bitch. I don't hate you. I just can't stand yo' ass."

When she said that, I wanted to slap her badly. She didn't have a reason to feel that way about me. I did everything that I was told to do, never talked back, and went to school every day without complaining. What more did she want from me?

"No, I have the right to question you about the things that you have done and said to me. I've been walking around you my whole life on eggshells. I have been the ideal child that anyone would have loved to have. I have never been in trouble in any way and I obeyed all the rules that you bestowed upon me. I've never even questioned anything you said up until now. I get recognition for all of my accomplishments from everyone but you. I graduated two weeks ago and received the highest honor in my graduating class, but my own mama was not in the building to congratulate me! What parent doesn't want to see their child succeed?"

She stood in the doorway glaring at me as if I had cursed her out. The veins protruding from her forehead and her eyebrows were damn near touching. Pulling a Newport cigarette from her breast along with a lighter, she placed it to her lips.

"That shit didn't mean a damn thing to me!" she said after blowing the smoke out of her mouth.

"What the fuck was I congratulating you for? I didn't graduate high school, so it was nothing to me. It's not like you're going to college anyway. You ain't gon' be shit just like me. Yo' ass will be right here living in the projects and having babies like all the rest of the hoes around here. Is that what your attitude's about, me not going to your graduation and you not going to college?" she asked, laughing.

I couldn't believe she opened her mouth and let those words spew out. Then again, this was Dot I was talking about. She was lowkey jealous because I thrived without her help. I accomplished way more than she had ever did and I was only seventeen. Graduating wasn't in her plans for me and success was something I was never supposed to achieve. The shit was sad and I was beyond livid because the truth had come out, at least some of it.

"Let me get this straight. You didn't support me throughout my life because of what you didn't do back in the day? As a parent, you are supposed to want your child to be better than you! Not tear them down! That's the most selfish shit I have ever heard in my life!" I didn't mean to curse but I was mad.

Slap!

My head whipped to the side, leaving my face stinging. Tears welled up in my eyes but I refused to let them fall. As I focused on the photo of my best friend Poetry and I that hung on the wall, I took a deep breath and turned my head to give her my undivided attention. I was far from done speaking my piece. The answers to all my questions would be answered, she owed me that much.

"Putting your hands on me is not going to stop me from saying what I have to say, Dot. I will not be like the other girls around here that don't want to do anything with their lives. I didn't work my ass off in school to stop at a high school diploma. I want more for myself and being a statistic on welfare living in the projects is not one of my goals. As far as college goes, what makes you think I'm not going?"

I couldn't wait to hear what her rebuttal would be for that. I hadn't gotten one acceptance letter, but I knew I had applied to many colleges. With the grades I had throughout school, there was no way not one college wanted me at their school.

"How many college letters have you got? There hasn't been one piece of mail that has come here for you. That's how I know your ass ain't going anywhere. The way it's looking, you wasn't working too hard in school. I don't know how in the hell you were going to pay for it anyway. Do I look like I have money to put you through school?"

Her response made me chuckle. "See the thing about that is this, I haven't received any responses at *this* address," I said, pointing toward the floor. "I've put in so many college applications and I haven't seen one response. Not because they didn't come, but because you never gave them to me! It's ironic that the one school that I wanted to attend accepted me. When I called to inquire about my application, they told me I called just in time because my deadline was three days away. I explained to them that I never received the letter. Oh, how wrong I was. They told me the address that they sent it to and when. You didn't give it to me! But don't worry, I straightened it out."

"Yeah, I got the damn letters, I can't afford to send you to college. I'm not about to go broke trying to put you through school."

"I haven't asked you to do a damn thing for me! If I had to depend on you to do any fucking thing for me, I'd be waiting. You don't care about me, you never have. I've had to fend for myself almost my whole life. I got myself where I am today, not Dorothy Morrison. Me, Kaymee Shanice Morrison! So, fuck all that shit you talking right now, I'm gonna make sure I'm good like I've been doing." I said glaring in her eyes.

"Don't ever disrespect me like that! Who the fuck do you think you are, cursing in my damn house? Let along at me! You must be out of your mind, bitch!" she yelled, standing over me waiting to strike again.

"You may as well get your fist ready because I'm about to say everything that's on my mind. You had my life panned for failure, but since I've overcome every obstacle thus far, you still won't support me? You have me out here pegged to be a baby mama and I'm not even sexually active! It hurts me to the core that I don't have the backing of the one person that matters, my mother! But just to let you know, I don't need your support. I'll be okay. If speaking my mind is being disrespectful, oh well. You've been disrespecting me every day of my life, but my truth made you feel some type of way."

I was so mad that I was shaking. I couldn't believe the things that she said, then for her to smack me like I was in the wrong. I had to get out of that house before I punched her ass. Raising up from the bed, I went to my closet to choose an outfit for the day. All the while, my mom was still standing in the doorway watching my every move.

"Just because you graduated from high school doesn't mean that you are grown. Now, back to some of the shit that you touched on in your little speech. I highly doubt your ass is a virgin, so you can save that for someone that don't know any better. You ain't never in this house, so I know you be laid up somewhere."

"When I'm not here, I'm at work. When I'm not at work, I was at school. But you don't have to worry about where I'm at when I'm not here. I'd rather be anywhere other than this house any day," I said, taking a pair of white denim shorts off the hanger before throwing them on the bed.

I chose a pink t-shirt that had the word "beautiful" across the chest and tossed that on top of my shorts. Dot was still standing there watching me. I wish she would go sit down somewhere. I was done going back and forth with her.

"When you come in tonight, I want my rent money. If you don't have it, you better do whatever it takes to get it. And I do mean anything."

She was trying to push me in a corner so she could put me out, but I had money saved that she didn't know about. My granny taught me to never let the left hand know what the right hand was doing. I have been working since I was fourteen years old. Babysitting, walking dogs, sitting with old people, and tutoring. At sixteen, I started working as a cashier at Walmart. I worked when I got out of school almost every day because I hated being at home. I worked so hard that I had gotten a couple raises since I'd been there. That gave me the opportunity to save money as well as shop on a budget.

I walked the short distance to the dresser and opened the top drawer without acknowledging the ignorant shit that she just spewed. I retrieved a pair of pink boy shorts and the matching bra. Grabbing my clothes off the bed, I walked toward the door to go to the bathroom. Dot glared at me with a scowl on her face.

"Where the fuck do you think you're going? You are not about to go out of this room with those little ass shorts on! My man is here," she yelled with a scowl on her face. I reached to my left, opened my dresser drawer, and pulled out a pair of joggers. I pulled them on and stared her in the eyes.

"Better?" I asked smartly.

She gave my body a once over and moved to the side. I guess I passed her inspection. As I made my way to the bathroom, I passed her room and the door was opened. There was an ashy nigga laying in her bed with his dick in his hand. She didn't even have the decency to close the door when she left out. If she cared anything about me, she would have made sure I wouldn't have seen his ass, period. I walked into the bathroom and slammed the door as hard as I could.

"Slam another door in my house like you pay the bills and watch me fuck you up!" she screamed from somewhere in the apartment.

Laughing to myself, I turned the water on in the sink and grabbed my toothbrush. "I do pay the bills around this mufucka. That's why yo' ass all in my pockets," I mumbled to myself.

I spent the next twenty minutes getting my hygiene together. I applied makeup to my face to hide the handprint that stood out on the left side. I settled for a light powder foundation because it was supposed to hit eighty degrees. I took the scarf off my head and sprayed oil on my locs. I went to the salon and had them twisted and pinned up the night before.

When I exited the bathroom, lil' ashy was standing outside the door. My skin started itching immediately. He looked like a crack head and scratched like one, too. His hair was matted on one side and his teeth were yellow as hell. He smelled like they had been fucking all night. Nigga smelling like ass, dick, and pussy. That shit had me feeling sick to my stomach.

"Damn, you fine. I see why yo' mama can't stand yo' pretty ass, she ain't got shit on you, ma."

He stood back licking his lips and stroking his dick through his dirty pants. I practically ran to get away from him. Before I could step in my room, I heard him say something that stopped me in my tracks.

"I bet that lil' pussy could grip my dick just right."

I looked back at him slit-eyed. "And that would be the moment you take your last breath, nigga," I shot back, entering my room. I slammed the door hard enough to shatter every window in the apartment.

"Nasty ass nigga. I wish he would put his hands on me," I mumbled.

I went to my closet and grabbed my pink and white-strapped sandals. Putting them on, I picked up my phone and texted my best friend Poetry. I let her know that I was on my way to her house. I didn't feel safe in this bitch and I knew I had to get a lock for my door. I would figure out how to install it my damn self.

I grabbed my purse and walked out of my room. The aroma of breakfast was in the air, hitting me in the face as soon as I stepped out into the hall. I knew Dot didn't make enough for me, but I was going to fuck with her anyway. "Where my plate at?" I asked, looking between her and ashy dude when I walked in the kitchen.

"I didn't make none for you. Until you can respect me, you're on your own. I asked you nicely not to slam no muthafuckin' doors in my house, but you did the shit twice already as well as cussin'," she said, taking a bite of her bacon.

The shit she said was ludicrous. I couldn't even stop myself from giggling. "I've been taking care of myself for the past few years, in case you forgot. Anyway, you mean to tell me that Mr. Pedophile over there can eat but your daughter can't?" I asked, pointing at her dude. "It's cool. Just tell *your man* to stay away from me and that's the last time I'm going to say it." I turned to walk out of the apartment and Dot was on my heels.

"What you mean by that?" she asked with an attitude.

"Ask your man. I gotta find something to do with my life," I said snidely.

I walked down the piss smelling hallway to the staircase because the elevator wasn't working. I could still hear them arguing as I skipped down the stairs making sure I didn't touch anything. I hated living in the projects because the building that we lived in was always nasty. Everything from condoms to shit was always lying around as if that's how it was supposed to be.

When I stepped out of the building, I noticed the weather was nice. It was the end of May and the sun was shining brightly with a light breeze. The summer heat hadn't taken over yet. There were a couple of niggas standing around outside waiting for the fiends to come through to score drugs from them. That was the norm in my neighborhood, a lot of people that did nothing for a living.

"What's up, Kaymee? Yo' lil' ass growing up and you fine as hell. When you gon' let me take you out?"

"I got you on February thirtieth, I promise," I said, without looking his way. I didn't know who he was, but he was always around. I just never paid any attention to the things he said whenever he tried to talk to me. He had nothing to offer me standing in front of the building all day, every day. There were plenty of females around the neighborhood willing to bust it open for him, but I wasn't one of them.

"I'm gonna hold you to that, shawty."

"Please do," I said and laughed. "I'll be ready."

"Nigga, yo' ass should've stayed in school. You just got played," one of his homies said, laughing.

"I didn't get played, nigga. I'm waiting on that. She pure as fuck," I heard him say.

"Nigga, the month of February don't even have thirty fuckin' days! Stupid ass."

I turned the corner laughing my ass off, leaving them to argue that situation out. And he wondered why I wouldn't give him any play. There you have it. That would be a mistake waiting to happen and I wasn't about to set myself up like that. I was good with the problems I already had. I didn't have room for more.

Chapter 2
Poetry

I was sitting outside on my front porch waiting on my best friend Kaymee to walk down the street. When she called to tell me that she was on her way to my house, that only meant Dot was on her bullshit again. I hated my girl had to deal with the shit her mama put her through.

She didn't have to put up with it too much longer because we were out of this bitch in a couple months. Both of us were accepted to Spelman and we were lucky enough to share a dorm. I was so excited my bestie was going to be in Atlanta with me. I wondered if that was why Dot was tripping.

It was a shame that Kaymee had to have all her college mail sent to my house. When she told me that she hadn't gotten any acceptance letters from any of the colleges, I found it odd. Her grades were beyond immaculate, so I knew she should've had a full ride.

I couldn't let her give up that easily, so I told her to call every college that she applied to. Low and behold, she was accepted to all eighty-three of them. When I say my girl could go to any college and she didn't have to pay for anything, it was true.

I was so proud of her and so were my parents. It took determination and dedication for her to graduate with a four point three GPA, all without the support of her mother. My parents were at our graduation, cheering both of us on because her mother didn't show up. Shit, she didn't even pay any of her fees. Kaymee worked her ass off to pay for everything, including prom. My mom offered to help her, but she wanted to do it on her own and she did.

My phone began to ring. It was my boyfriend, Montez. The biggest smile appeared on my face as I listened to his ringtone blare out of the phone. I answered before it stopped ringing.

"Hey, baby," I sang.

"What took you so long to answer, Poetry?" he asked with an attitude

"I was listening to the song that plays when you call my phone. What's going on?" I asked since he had an attitude. I wasn't in the mood to be lovey dovey anymore.

"I was trying to find out what you had going on for the day."

"None of your fucking business," is what I wanted to say but instead, I answered his question.

"I didn't have anything planned. Kaymee is on her way over. I'm waiting on her to walk up any minute."

He was talking to somebody but I couldn't make out what he was saying. I was getting irritated as fuck because he didn't say hold on for a second or shit.

"Monty! Who the hell are you over there whispering to, being all secretive and shit?" I asked loudly.

"Man, cut that out! I'm talking to my homie over here while you on that jealous ass shit. They' having a basketball tournament over at Seward Park. Won't y'all come through," he said.

"You coming to get us?" I asked, rolling my eyes.

"If I could, you know I would. I'm playing and won't have time to roll over there. Hop in a cab and I'll pay for it when y'all get here. I need my good luck charm so I can beat these niggas on this court."

"Alright, baby. I'll be there as soon as Kaymee gets here."

"I'll see you in a minute, sexy. I love you."

"I love you, too," I said before ending the call.

As soon as I glanced up from my phone, I saw Kaymee walking down the street. She had on a pair of white shorts that were hugging her thighs to death. The pink shirt she had on showed off her flat stomach, but what stood out the most was her locs. They were twisted from the bottom and pinned up. What made it look so good was the fact that the locs on top hung to one side and they were crinkled and dyed red.

Kaymee was light bright, damn near white and the color fit her perfectly. She stood five foot five inches and she was about a hundred forty pounds. She had ass, titties, and a small waist. My best friend was beautiful.

I myself was five feet seven and petite. I had very long silky hair that I got from my mama. Everyone called us Salt and Pepper because I was dark-skinned and she was light-skinned. We always laughed at that because we always listen to old *Salt & Pepa* music.

"Hey, bestie! What it do, pimpin'?" she yelled when she was a few yards from my house.

She knew not to do that shit in front of my crib because my mama didn't play that. I waved at her and she started laughing because she knew I wanted to scream but couldn't. I got up and ran down the steps and straight to her.

"Best friend! I'm so happy to see you right now!" I screamed.

Smacking her lips, she said, "We need to find something to get into because I'm not for sitting on that damn porch all day."

"That's not what we will be doing today. Monty called and said they're having a basketball tournament at Seward Park. That's where we are going, to watch my man play ball. Girl, there are gonna be some fine ass niggas out there. Maybe you can find a damn man to lose that thang to."

"Whatever. When the hell did Monty get back? It seems like I haven't seen him in so long."

Monty was two years older than us. When he graduated from high school, he went on to continue his education at Morehouse. That was the reason I chose Spelman. I wanted to be close to my man. I saw him often because every chance he got, he was back in Chicago.

"He came in the day before yesterday, but I haven't seen him. I've talked to him often, though. Today will be my first time laying eyes on him. I missed my baby, too."

"I can't wait to see his crazy ass. What time are we leaving? And how are we getting there?" she asked.

We walked up the steps and into the house. "As soon as I tell my mom what's up, we out," I said, heading in the direction of the kitchen.

"Tell me what, Poetry? I hope you don't think you're getting my car. I have things to do," she said, still cutting an onion.

My mom could be feisty at times, but she was a sweetheart. Our relationship was one of the best but she would get in my ass quickly if need be. My daddy saved me most of the times when he felt she was being too hard on me.

"I'm not trying to get the car, ma. I wanted to tell you that Kaymee and me are going to Seward Park. There's a basketball tournament and Monty's playing. He's paying for a cab."

My mom was beautiful. She was forty years old and didn't look a day over thirty. Many have said that we look like twins, except she wore her hair short. We had a relationship where we could talk about everything. She listened to what I brought to her but didn't hesitate to voice her opinion on the matter. That was one of the reasons why our relationship was so strong. She didn't judge me.

She turned around, wiping her hands on a paper towel. "Oh. Hi, Kaymee. I didn't know you were here. How you doing, baby?" she asked, smiling.

My parents loved them some Kaymee. They tried their best to show her the love that she wasn't getting at home. They didn't want her to get lost in the streets.

"I'm fine, Mama Chris. How are you?"

"I can't complain. Thanks for asking. Aren't you looking all cute and stuff," she said, flicking her locs.

"Now, about this tournament. I'm gonna let y'all go, but be careful. Them fools been acting up lately and its summertime. So y'all know how that goes," she said, looking back and forth between the two of us.

"Yeah, we know how it is, and I will call home if anything happens," I said.

"Same here," Kaymee said, looking at my mom.

My mom kept looking at Kaymee with a perplexed expression on her face. I didn't know why she was staring her down like that. It made me glance over to see if I could figure it out, but I couldn't.

"Ma, what are you staring at?"

Instead of answering, she walked the short distance to where Kaymee was standing. My mom raised her hand and rubbed her fingers across Kaymee's face. The scowl that appeared on my mom's face alarmed me. I only saw that look when she was pissed and that wasn't very often. Kaymee tried to hold her head down, but my mom wasn't having it.

"Kaymee, I'm going to ask you one time, and one time only. What happened to your face?"

I didn't see what my mom was seeing. When we were outside, I didn't notice anything either. Maybe when I hugged her some of her makeup came off. Shit, I didn't know.

"My mom slapped me, but it's okay," she said lowly.

"It's not okay! I can't tell her ass how to treat her child, but you don't have to put up with her shit! I want you to know that you are welcomed here anytime. If you feel that you don't want to be there, you can always come here. You will be eighteen in a few weeks, old enough to make your own decisions. Something that you've been doing since I've known you. Call me. My door is always open to you."

The tears that streamed down Kaymee's cheeks ran her makeup. That's when I notice the red mark on the left side of her face. I moved slowly to her side and wrapped my arms around her as she cried.

"It's almost over, chica. It's almost over. Everything will be alright. I'm gonna be here every step of the way. You are not alone as long as you have me," I whispered in her ear. "Dry them tears so we can get the hell outta here."

We both laughed out loud. Wiping the tears from her eyes, she turned to my mom and smiled. She sniffed a couple times and held her head high.

"Thank you so much. I'll keep what you said in mind, but there are so many questions that Dot must answer for me. I received some of those answers today, but I need to know everything. After I get what I need, she won't have to worry about seeing me again."

Kaymee gave my mom a hug and walked down the hall to the bathroom. Me and my mom stood quietly for a few minutes without speaking. Honestly, I didn't know what to say.

"Did she tell you what happened?" my mom asked.

I shook my head no. "I knew something happened because she called me saying she was on her way over. We didn't make any plans before she came over. She didn't say anything about why she left home either," I explained to my mom.

"I hope she gets away from the negativity that her mom is always bestowing upon her soon. When I say soon, I don't mean when she leaves for school either. Dot has ruined that child and Kaymee is trying her best not to let it show. But she has to keep the positive attitude that she has always had," my mom said, shaking her head. "That's all I have to say about the matter. Be careful out there, Poetry. I love you."

My mom left the kitchen and went upstairs. I knew she was upset. She always became that way when it came to Kaymee. She loved my best friend and wanted the best for her.

Kaymee came back from the bathroom. Her face didn't show any signs that she had been crying. The mark on her face was unseen, as well.

"I called for a cab while I was in the bathroom. It will be here in about five minutes. Let's go have fun, boo," she said, hitting me on the arm and walking to the door.

Chapter 3
Montez

"We got the court when these busta ass niggas finish. The black team gettin' that ass spanked! They need to hurry up and lose because I'm ready to show these fools how a real muthafucka play."

"Nigga, the last time I checked, Morehouse ain't won shit since the nineties. Stick to academics nigga. We are gonna slaughter your team," this lil'nigga said, chuckling.

See, that muthafucka got it twisted. I'm at Morehouse for what the fuck I can learn. I play ball to keep in shape. My baller skills came from right there in those projects, street ball. That's how some of these muthafuckas end up getting their feelings hurt, thinking because I went off to school, shit changed. Nah I'm still the same muthafucka, just a little polished.

"Save all that ying yang shit for the court, nigga. As a matter of fact, if yo' ass so confident about winning put yo' money where ya mouth is. I got five hunnid on it. What'd you say?" I said, going in my pocket pulling out my money.

"Nigga, you had to work hard for that money. My shit stays rolling in on a daily. So that lil' shit ain't nothing. Let's do it," he said, pulling his money out.

"I'll hold that shit. Winner takes all," my homie Dray said, walking over.

"This shit was gonna be like taking candy from a baby." I laughed to myself. I looked towards the parking lot and saw my baby getting out of a cab. "I'll be right back. I gotta take care of something," I said to Dray.

"Don't go too far. There's money on the line. Get ready to run my paper."

The dude I had bet on the game with was still running his mouth. I didn't even respond to his ass because everything I had to say, would be said on the court. Jogging where the cab was parked, I paid the driver and grabbed my baby around her waist. I looked down at her and fell in love all over again. Poetry was always so beautiful to me.

I met her when she stepped into Jones College Prep High School four years ago. Her lil' feisty ass turned me on with every word that came out of her mouth. I knew I had to have her and I got her, too.

She was always shading a nigga, playing hard to get, but I broke that ass down. One day I came to school prepared for her smart mouth. I saw her walking down the hall with Kaymee, laughing and smiling. She was wearing a pair of jeans that hugged her small frame just right. I squared my shoulders and walked up to her.

"Hey, Poetry. How's your day so far?" I asked her.

"It's like any other day when I'm at school," she said, rolling her eyes.

She tried to keep walking but I stepped in front of her, blocking her path. She glanced at her friend and started laughing. I didn't know what the hell was so amusing, but she was about to find out I wasn't one of these lil' niggas that didn't know any better.

"What's funny about what I said, Poetry?" I asked.

"Every day you step to me and I curve your ass every day. What's it gonna take to get you to understand that I'm not feeling you, Monty?" she said, walking around me. "Come on, Kaymee. Let's go."

I watched her walk away and chuckled. I'd never had a girl that wasn't interested in me. Shit, I was six feet tall, light-skinned, handsome, and I played ball. I also knew how to treat a girl like the queen that she was destined to be. There was no way I was about to let her dismiss me like that.

"Poetry, hold up!" I called after her.

She paused for a second but kept going. I let her go, but she would be mine before the day was over. When school was out, I went outside to wait on the steps until she came out the doors. Kaymee emerged first and Poetry wasn't far behind. That beautiful smile that I fell in love with was displayed on her face. When she saw me, the irritated expression she threw at me was cute.

"Today is the day you are gon' stop trying to play me, ma. I'm trying to get to know you on a   different level."

"I don't want—."

I cut her words off before she could start her bullshit. "Right now, it's not about what you want. I wanna be your man and that's all that matters right now. I'll treat you like you've never been treated before. I got plans for you, Poetry baby," I said, reaching in my pocket.

I went out and bought her a silver necklace that had a P and M charm surrounded in diamond chips. That's how confident I was that I would get what I wanted. I wasn't trying to buy her love. The gesture was to let her know that I went all out for mine. I opened the jewelry box and held it out to her.

"Poetry, would you be my lady?" I asked.

Smacking her lips, she shot back, "What did I tell you earlier, Monty? Get out of here with that weak shit."

"Girl, stop fronting! This nigga is all you been talking about since we stepped foot in this school. From the first time you laid eyes on him, you couldn't wait to say some slick shit about him. Girl, he is fine and a gentleman. Give him a chance," Kaymee said, putting her on blast.

Poetry tried to act like she was mad, but I knew she wasn't. Her eyes didn't look at the gift, but they never left mine. I knew she was about to cave.

She agreed to go out with me a couple times, and we have been together ever since.

"Hey, baby. I've missed you so much," I said, kissing her deeply.

"Ummm, hello! That shit is so rude, Monty. You could've said hi before you started molesting my bestie in public."

I finished milking my baby for all her sweetness then turned to Kaymee's lil' hating ass. She'd been cock blocking too damn long. I came home prepared for her ass. I brought my boy Drayton with me. I had plans to introduce the two of them and see where it went from there. She would not block the time I spent with Poetry this time around.

"Yo, Mee. Listen, my lil' nigglet. I have to address my Queen before I utter a word to the peasants." I laughed as I dodged the right hook she threw at me. "Nah, for real. Get yo' ass over here and give me a hug," I said, opening my arms.

She walked over to me and I towered over her short ass. Kaymee was like my lil' sis. I looked out for her even when I was away at school. I was glad that both of them were coming down to Atlanta. Now I wouldn't have to worry about her so much. The things that she had been going through were constantly on my mind.

"I got somebody I want you to meet. Come on. I have to be on the court in about ten minutes," I said as we walked back to the park.

I saw Dray talking to a chubby chic that was smiling in his face. He didn't seem like he was too interested but he stood listening to the conversation. He looked up and saw us walking in his direction and his eyes never went back to the chic. He knew who Poetry was from seeing her on Facetime when we talked, the recognition of Kaymee from the many photos that I showed him from her social media page.

I shot him a sly smirk and he nodded his head with approval. I looked over at Kaymee but she was looking around nervously. She had always been timid. I think it had a lot to do with her bitch ass mama. But I was trying to get her to live a little, have some fun. Shit, she was about to go off to college. She had to loosen up.

When we got to where Dray was standing, the chubby chic caught an instant attitude. It was written all over her face. She rolled her eyes and tried to continue the conversation, but Dray had counted her ass out three minutes prior. He only had eyes for Kaymee at that point.

"How the fuck you gonna be all in the next bitch face when you're standing here with me?" she snapped.

Poetry's set on go ass was trying to get at the girl but I closed my hand tightly around hers. Glancing down at her with a "don't play with me" look, she calmed her ass down. She knew I didn't play that fighting shit. She was too damn fine for all that.

Dray pried his eyes away from Kaymee and stared down at the chick. He didn't seem happy about what she said. She tried to pick the conversation up but he wasn't trying to hear shit she had to say. Throwing his hand up in her face, he looked her square in the eyes.

"First of all, you came over here to me. I didn't invite you over here. You did that voluntarily. Secondly, I don't know you, so you can stop acting like we rock like that. Thirdly, watch ya tongue   because ain't no bitches in the vicinity. Now that I know how much of a hothead you are, you can move around, shawty. That shit ain't attractive at all. But I see something that I *do* want to get to know, so you are free to go about your day," he said, licking his lips as he turned to looked at Kaymee.

Baby girl was pissed because he dissed her ass intelligently. "Fuck you, nigga. You ain't all that anyway," she said, stomping off.

I couldn't do nothing but laugh because his ass was wild for that shit. But that was Dray for you. Walking over to Kaymee, he draped his arm around her shoulder and said, "Hey, beautiful. I'm Dray." Me and Poetry walked to the court, leaving them to get acquainted.

Dray was a good guy and I wasn't saying that because he was my boy. I wouldn't even bring him to meet Mee if I didn't think he wouldn't do right by her. Dray and I already had the big brother talk and you best believe he knew that I took my sister's feelings into consideration. If they were hurt, it better had been for a damn good reason. He agreed to what I was saying after I explained all the do's and don'ts to him.

I met Dray the minute I stepped into our dorm room at Morehouse College. I was geeked as hell to be going to a well-known school that everyone had nothing but good things to say about it. I was finally away from the projects and was ready to start a new life without guns, drugs and violence. Being in Atlanta to attend school was my second chance to do right.

"What's up, man? I'm Drayton, but you can call me Dray. Don't ask, I don't know what the hell my mama was thinking when she named me that shit."

Giving him a head nod, I walked over to the bed that was obviously for me. I wasn't one to get close with any nigga at first sight. Where I came from, it was best to feel a muthafucka out before you get all buddy buddy with their ass. Everybody started out as a foe until I decided they were good enough to become a friend.

"I'm Montez, but you can call me Monty. I figured I'd give you that bit of information since we gotta live in this bitch together. I don't know you and you don't know me. What I'm saying is this. Don't touch my shit and I won't touch yours. I prefer you ask me for what you want because if some shit come up missing, I'm fucking you up. I'm a private muthafucka, so don't have any and everybody in here cause again, if something come up missing, I'm fucking you up."

He stood there I guess trying to figure me out. It wasn't going to happen. The only way he was   going to get to know me was by sitting back and observing how I moved. I still didn't believe he would get it right going that route. He looked like a lame ass nigga anyway, but I thought he was going to be cool. Time would tell though.

"Look, man. I'm the same way about my shit, too. I don't think we will have any problems in that department. Well, it's nice to meet you, Monty. I was just unpacking and getting my side of the room together. Would you like to go with me to the Walmart? I have to get a couple things that I didn't know I needed," he asked, taking clothes out of his luggage.

"Yeah, that's cool. I have to shop all together. I only brought clothes with me. This college shit wasn't in my plans until an OG got in my ear about leaving and doing something with my life. I'll see if this is the life for me or not."

I hung up all of my clothes in the cubby that was on my side of the room. I lined my shoes along the floor and put my toiletries on the shelf. Shit, that's all I had to put away. I kept looking from my side to his and knew that I had a lot of shit to buy to make this muthafucka home. It wouldn't be hard. All I had to do was go shopping.

"Oh, there's a box on the desk right there. I knew it wasn't for me because my name is not Mr. Williams. Is your last name, Williams?" he asked, putting more of his things away.

"Yeah, that's me," I said, walking to the desk by the window. Looking down at the package, I knew what was in the box without opening it. I addressed that muthafucka myself before I sent it. The United Parcel Service better hope it still contained what the fuck I put in it, too.

I used my key to cut the tape that was holding the box closed. I smiled when I saw the top of the safe in the box. It was about two feet high and fire resistant. It was good enough for what I needed it for. I ripped the rest of the box from around the safe and threw it to the side. I was trying to see if my shit was still inside. I knew it was because I had already set up the code and everything beforehand. I lifted the safe, as heavy as it was, placing it in the middle compartment of my cubby. I pushed it all the way to the back and entered the code.

Smiling from ear to ear, I ran my hand over the stacks of bills that I had banded together. Yeah, I wasn't your average college student. I was a muthafuckin' boss. Making sure everything else was in place, I grabbed a couple stacks and closed the safe door, pulling the handle to make sure it was locked.

"Hey, Monty. I'm almost ready to head out. You ready? And what the hell you need a safe for, fam?"

With my back to him, I put both stacks in each of my front pockets. I turned around and stared at him hard. "Mind ya business, man. What did I tell you about my side of the room? Anything going on over here, is none of yo' concern. Now, when you're ready, we can go."

That was the day a brotherhood was born. Dray had driven his whip to school, so we had transportation to and from. We headed out to find the shit that we needed. This dude was pushing a black 2009 Navigator fully loaded. We were sitting at the light listening to the GPS guide us to our destination. Out of the blue, a nigga was on the driver's side of the car, pointing a .38 in Dray's face.

I couldn't believe this shit. I didn't think about bringing my burner that was tucked away in the safe back at the dorm. If I would've known that Morehouse was sitting damn near around the corner from the hood, a nigga would've been strapped.

"Get out the muthafuckin' truck, nigga!" the dude said, pushing the gun into Dray's temple.

Looking out the side mirror, I noticed there wasn't one car behind us. I was told that the streets of Atlanta stayed jam packed, but I guess everybody decided to stay in the crib that day. We were literally the only people on the street and there was no way anybody could save us.

"Okay, man. Be cool, I'll get out. Just take the truck. No one needs to get hurt. This shit ain't worth dying for," Dray said to the gunman.

"Shut the fuck and get out! I don't need to hear that pussy shit you talkin' right now! Get the fuck out the truck, nigga!"

Dray reached to open the door. I noticed his hand was going for something he had tucked away in the door. At that moment, dude turned his head for whatever reason and Dray sent that nigga to meet his maker. He let him have it point blank in the back of his head with no hesitation. Peeling off, he cut a right and headed back to the dorm. All I could say was this, we didn't go shopping that day and we got rid of the truck, too.

MEESHA

Chapter 4
Kaymee

When Monty said that he had someone he wanted me to meet, I knew I wouldn't be interested but I was willing. While we were walking back to the park, my eyes browsed the area trying to make sure there wasn't anything out of the ordinary going on. Something could happen at a drop of a dime in Chicago and I wanted to be ready.

There were plenty of people out that day and everyone was having a good time. It was good to see the kids out having fun and enjoying the weather. Someone brought a grill out and the food smelled good as hell. It made me remember I hadn't eaten anything before I left home.

I turned and locked eyes with the finest man I'd ever seen. He was six feet tall, dark brown complexion, low haircut, and built like a God. He was standing next to a girl that he stopped paying attention to when we started walking in his direction. His eyes followed every step I took. I felt my face getting hot from blushing. There wasn't anything wrong with looking, but that's as far as it would go.

The chic started going off, talking reckless as hell as we got closer. Mr. Fine broke eye contact and checked her ass quickly. Anyone that knew me already knew the "bitch" word didn't faze me at all. I grew up thinking that was my name, so whenever someone called me "bitch", I smiled.

Poetry, on the other hand, was ready to pounce on her ass, but the grip Monty had on her hand prevented her from doing so. She stared at him like she was gonna say something, but the glare he shot at her made her swallow her words.

After ol' girl stormed off mad at the world, Mr. Fine walked over to me, draped his arm around my shoulders, and smiled.

"Hey, beautiful. I'm Dray," he said, looking down at me. "What's your name, cutie?"

"Kaymee," was all I said as I shrugged his arm off me.

He was cute and all, but I wasn't looking for a companion. I'd been without a boyfriend all my life. I wasn't trying to have one either. I didn't know what he thought was going to happen with us, but in my mind, it was a no for me on everything. His smile was so perfect. I had to look away before I found myself lost in it.

"That's a pretty name. Why you running from a nigga?"

"I'm not running. I just don't like when people that I don't know touch me," I explained, walking ahead of him.

I made it to the court first, glimpsing around the area. The bleachers were almost full and I wanted to sit in the front. I spotted a space that would be big enough for the both Poetry and I, and headed straight for it. I sat down and ignored the intensive stare that Dray was giving me. He followed me to the bench and watched my every move. Once I sat down, I looked everywhere but at him. I gave the indication of not wanting to be bothered, but he didn't get the hint.

"Damn, you just gon' ignore me? I wanna get to know you, ma. I see I'm gon' have to come   correct or not at all, huh?" I didn't respond to what he was saying, but that didn't stop him from continuing to talk. "It's alright. I'll leave you alone for now. We got all summer to make this right."

I looked up at him stoned-faced and still didn't respond. He took that as his cue to get away from me. He walked back to where Poetry and Monty were hugged up with each other.

"Yo, Monty. Your team is up!" one of the refs yelled out.

Monty kissed Poetry on the lips and walked onto the court. She headed straight for me and sat down. Dray jogged back to where we were, reaching in his pocket.

"Fam said hold this, Poe," he said, handing her a knot of rolled up bills.

"What the —"

"Just hold it, no questions. Put it away," he said, pulling up his basketball shorts as he walked away.

Poetry peered in Monty's direction and he nodded his head. She put the money in her purse and we sat waiting for the game to start. There were plenty of fine men out and just as many thirsty women.

"What do you think about Dray?" she asked, glancing at me.

"He's cute, but I don't know anything about him other than that. I can sense that he is a ladies man and with that comes drama. I'm good on that shit. One thing I'm not about to do is compete over a man."

She rolled her eyes and waved me off. "Nobody said you had to marry the nigga, Kaymee. I'm glad my boo brought someone to meet you. Loosen your ass up before we hit the south," she said, laughing.

I didn't find anything funny. The way my home life was set up, I wasn't trying to have anyone new in my circle. That would only give Dot another reason to think I was out fucking every damn body. I'd rather not give her anything to speculate about.

"I don't know him!" I said, getting frustrated.

"Don't get mad. I got you. His name is Drayton Montgomery. He is from Pittsburgh, Pennsylvania and he goes to Morehouse. Monty said that he doesn't have a woman. I can tell that he liked what he saw when he laid eyes on you."

"Why are you telling me all this? I'm really not interested in getting to know him, Poetry. That's the last thing I need to worry about. I just want to enjoy my summer," I explained.

"Whatever you say, best friend," she said as she watched the referee throw the ball in the air, letting us know the game was underway.

Monty's team wore black jerseys and the other team had on red ones. The black team started the game off with a three pointer, shot by Monty. Before long, the score was thirty-two to twenty, our way. The red team was playing very aggressively and the game was getting physical.

For some reason, my eyes couldn't stay off Dray. The sweat that was rolling down his face and arms had my kitty tingling. He was even sexier wet. I couldn't help licking my lips, the sight of him was making me thirsty. The feelings I felt in my lower region was something I had never felt before. I was kind of nervous about it.

Dray stole the ball from the guy that he was guarding and took off down the court. He went up for a dunk and a tall guy from the red team forcibly pushed him from behind as he went up. Dray went crashing to the ground, hard. Monty and the other black team members went straight for the dude. That's when the fight started. There were punches being thrown from every direction. The referees couldn't get the guys under control. Everyone stood on their feet waiting to see what would happen next, but not one person tried to stop the fight.

"Oh shit!" Poetry yelled, jumping to her feet.

I was nervous as hell because once a fight broke out, that's when the bullets started flying. I noticed that Dray had gotten up in the midst of the fists that were being thrown. The scene before me looked like a Royal Rumble match. One of the refs grabbed Monty and pulled him away. As soon as he did, the police came from every direction with their guns drawn.

"Get the fuck down, now!" one of the officers yelled.

Monty snatched away from the ref that held him, running to grab Dray so he wouldn't get into trouble with the police. When he got to him, I don't know what the officer thought Monty was doing. He reached out and wrapped his arm around his neck, throwing him to the ground. The officer was trying to force his arm behind his back.

"What the fuck, man! I was only trying to get my dude! Get the fuck off me!" Monty yelled as he struggled to get his arms loose.

"Shut the fuck up! You going to jail, boy!" the officer yelled in his face.

"Jail? For what? Man, this some bullshit! You muthafuckas forever trying to lock a nigga up, pussy ass pigs!"

Monty was trying to get his arms free while the officer was trying to get his cuffs out. He was looking around for help when Monty freed himself. He didn't try to run or anything. Still, the officer hit him in the back of his head with his fist. Monty's head hit the pavement rather hard, causing him to look a little dazed.

"What the fuck!" Poetry yelled, running over to where Monty was being detained. I was right behind her.

"You don't have to put your hands on him! He's not even trying to get the fuck away! So why do you have to use force?" she screamed at the officer.

"Get your black ass back, bitch, before you go to jail with him!" he yelled.

"Bae, get back! Let this muthafucka do what he gon' do. I don't need you getting locked up, too," Monty said, putting his hands behind his back voluntarily.

Everybody in the park was now on the court. There were many with their cellphones out recording what was going on. I looked across the court and saw Dray hand-cuffed, sitting on the ground. He looked at me and smiled. I couldn't give him one in return because I was pissed about what this officer had done to Monty.

Another officer came over to assist with Monty, immediately putting his knee in his back. "That shit ain't even necessary! He is already down with his hands behind his back! The only thing you had to do was cuff him!" a guy yelled from behind me. "Don't worry, fam. I got every damn thing on camera. Stupid muthafuckas!"

The officer that had his knee in Monty's back cuffed him and stood up. He looked at the guy with the cellphone and started walking in his direction. He had the meanest scowl on his face. I was afraid he was going to do something to the guy. You couldn't be sure with these cops of today. They were always set to shoot a black man. I really wanted the guy and Monty to just comply with this officer, especially with him being such a hothead.

"Give me the damn phone!" the officer yelled.

"I'm not giving you shit! I paid for this! Get the fuck outta my face! It's not against the law to record this. You don't have anything to worry about anyway. This shit don't prove shit except the victim was right. Y'all ain't never proved wrong in these matters and y'all get to keep ya damn jobs."

"I'll have my eyes on you, boy," the officer sneered.

"Yeah? A'ight, muthafucka. I'm a grown ass man. Ain't no boy standing here! That man come home from college, now ya'll got him in handcuffs and for nothing. I hope the muthafuckas at Morehouse take y'all ass for every penny ya got," the guy said, still recording.

The officer looked somewhat worried by what the guy said. He turned and walked back to the center of the court, calling another officer over to him. They whispered back and forth, continuing to look at Monty. The officer that put his knee in Monty's back shook his head repeatedly. I looked over at Monty, the expression he had on his face was of pure rage. The way the officers treated him wasn't right. That was one of the reasons why black people didn't trust the police. They used their badges and guns to do us wrong.

"Mee, come here," Monty called out loud enough for me to hear.

I rushed to his side without drawing the attention of the police. "Are you okay? Did they hurt you in any way?" I asked him.

"Listen to me. We don't have time for that. Reach in my left pocket and get my keys. My wallet is in the armrest of the car and the pin number to my card is 8704. I'm gon' need you to go to the bank and get the money to bail me and Dray out. Tell Poetry to wait for my call. Y'all get out of here," he said sternly.

I retrieved the keys in the nick of time before the cop came over with more bullshit to spew out of his mouth. "Get the hell away from him! He doesn't need to talk to anyone!" he yelled.

"You can lower your voice because I didn't do anything to you, Officer Spencer," I said, looking at his name badge. "You should've been taught to respect others while you were in the academy," I said, walking away from him. I looked over my shoulder and he was still staring at me.

I walked briskly back to where Poetry was talking to the guy that recorded what happened. I caught the tail end of the conversation as he had sent her what he had to her phone. I was glad he had captured everything because the entire scenario was on some bullshit.

"Come on, Poetry. Monty wants us to leave and wait for his call. He gave me his keys and his pin number so we would be able to bail them out."

"I'm not leaving until I see them put him in the car. Did you see how they were handling him? That's why I hate these bitch ass cops!" she yelled.

"Poetry, take yo' ass home like I told you to! Get the fuck away from here!" Monty yelled at her from his position on the ground.

She looked at him with tears in her eyes and mouthed, "I love you." Monty nodded his headed towards his car, motioning us to leave. I glanced back at him and shot a look in Dray's direction before we walked off.

Poetry started crying. I tried to console her but she brushed me off and walked faster. I knew she was upset about what had happened. I was, too, but I decided to let her have her moment, following her to the parking lot.

***

"It's going to be okay, Poetry. Let's go and wait for Monty to call us," I said as we sat in Monty's car.

She refused to leave, so I didn't have a choice but to sit there and wait it out. I didn't have my license, so I couldn't drive away myself. We sat in the parking lot for another twenty minutes when we saw Monty walking across the park in our direction.

I sat up straight and Poetry opened the door, jumping out. She ran straight into his arms, burying her head in his chest. I let out a sigh of relief because they let him go.

As they walked to the car, I looked straight ahead and saw Dray walking our way. I don't know why I started smiling but I was happy that he was let go, as well. The many people that had their cameras out was probably the reason they were let go. The way the officers handled the situation was uncalled for.

Getting out of the front seat to get into the back, I looked at Poetry. I saw her frown was now replaced with a huge smile.

"How did they end up letting y'all go?" I asked Monty.

"I guess when Mike told that one officer that I went to Morehouse, he knew he had fucked up. All the extra shit they did was not necessary. I was already down and had stop tussling with his bitch ass, but his partner insisted on using force! They said I could go but before I left, I convinced them to let Dray go, as well."

Dray had a scowl on his face as he stepped in front of Monty. "Man, what the fuck was up with those niggas? That nigga tried to paralyze my ass. He was on some dirty ass shit. I bet not see that muthafucka again because when I do, I'm fuckin' him up, fam. He is lucky the law came. That's what saved his punk ass."

"I don't know what he was on, so I'm with you on that. Yeah, we had money riding on that game, but that was some hoe shit. They were getting their ass kicked and wanted to try to hurt some damn body. It's cool. We gon' see them again. They will be locked the fuck up for a minute. I got the winnings, so I'm good," Monty said, looking around the park.

The guys they were playing against went to jail from what Monty said. That eased my mind for the time being, because I knew it was going to be a problem down the line. Monty would be ready whenever they popped up again, and by the looks of things, Dray would be right beside him.

Monty didn't take things like that lightly. He was always getting in trouble when we were in school. When he told Poetry and I that he was going away for college, I told him that was a good idea. There were many guys on the streets that didn't like the way he was making moves. He didn't pay them any attention and they hated it.

"Let's go, baby. After all that's happened, I don't want to be out here anymore," Poetry said, getting in the car.

I sat in the backseat and buckled my seat belt. Dray got in on the driver's side and glanced my way. Acting as though I didn't see him, I put my ear buds in my ear. My stomach growled loudly. Monty turned around and started laughing. His mouth was moving but I didn't hear a word he said.

"What?" I asked, taking the ear bud out of my right ear.

"Yo' ass hungry as hell, huh?"

"I can't believe y'all heard that!" I exclaimed in embarrassment. "Yeah, I didn't eat before I left the house this afternoon. I was just trying to get the hell out of there before I beat Dot's ass. I'm so tired of her, man."

"What the fuck was she tripping about now?" Monty asked.

I really didn't want to tell him because I knew that he was going to get mad as hell. He hated the way Dot treated me and wanted to fuck her up a while ago, but that was still my mama. I couldn't let him do anything to her. Believe me, all I had to do was say "go" and he would be on her ass like white on rice.

"She came in my room calling me a bitch as usual. Then she started talking out the side of her neck, saying that I had to get out of her house and do something with my life. She said it as if all I do is lay around, I'm barely there as it is. When I am there, she finds something to fuck with me about. I asked her why she hated me so much, but she came back with a lot of fly shit. She's pissed because I surpassed her expectation of me being a fuck up. She actually said that I was going to be like all the hoes in the neighborhood, dumb and pregnant.

I was heated, repeating the things that Dot had said to me. The words themselves cut me deeply, but I knew I couldn't let her break me down. I climbed the ladder to where I was. She had nothing to do with any of that. I knew that I was going to have to be my biggest cheerleader and keep going.

"How did that come about? If she knew anything about you, she would know that you haven't had sex a day in your life!" Poetry yelled.

I wanted to hit her ass in the back of her head for putting my business out there. Monty knew everything about me. He was like a big brother, but that damn outburst made Dray grin like Chester Cheetah. I didn't need this negro thinking he would be getting anything over here.

"Damn, tell him my social security number while you're at it! That's not everybody's business, Poetry," I said, slumping back into the seat.

"That's not something to be ashamed of, Kaymee. Embrace that shit. But yo' mama is dead wrong for the shit, sis," Monty said, looking in the rearview mirror. "Let's get you something to eat. I got you. I promise."

He started the car and backed out of the parking space. My mind went back to that afternoon and the tears were threatening to fall. I heard Poetry talking but I didn't hear what she said. All of a sudden, Monty yelled out, "What the fuck is her problem, yo'? I'm telling you, Kaymee. Yo' mama is gonna be a distant muthafuckin' memory if she don't fall the fuck back! You will be eighteen years old and she still feels like she can treat you like a kid. Beat her ass if she put her hands on you again! I'm serious about that shit, on my mama."

I knew then that Poetry had said too much. She knew better than to tell his crazy ass about Dot slapping me. She looked back at me with the puppy eyes as I turned to look out the window. The scenes that passed as the car sped down the street were now blurred. I couldn't stop the tears that were cascading down my face.

Monty was holding the steering wheel tightly because his knuckles were damn near white. I felt as if him being upset was my fault. I couldn't blame Poetry because he should've heard that from me. Dray moved closer to me and wrapped me in his arms. The tears flowed at a rapid speed and he wiped every one of them.

"Everything will be alright, ma. You have to keep doing what you've been doing to succeed. I don't know what you are going through with your moms, but don't let her get under your skin. You are gonna get away from her and soar higher than you have ever done before," he whispered in my ear.

This was coming from someone that didn't know anything about me, but it didn't make me feel any better because I had yet to hear anything positive from the one person that mattered. I don't think that day would ever come, so I needed to push that shit to the back of my mind and keep my head up.

"Thank you, Dray. I appreciate that. Now, get off me," I said, shrugging him off.

"Well, at least I got the chance to hold you for a hot minute. That was good enough," he said, winking at me.

Monty pulled up to Dave & Buster's. All of the sadness that I was feeling went out of the window. This was my favorite place to be when I was down. Everything I felt always turned into a competitive war, which brought a smile to my face every time. I couldn't wait to get inside to let off some of the steam that I was holding in. Watching as Monty waited for his ticket from valet, Dray walked up to me.

"Are you ready to get beat in every game you touch?" He asked, licking his lips.

"In your dreams, pretty boy. I'd advise you to ask your homeboy about me. All I do is win. Remember that." I smiled at him.

He was cute and I would've liked to get to know him better, but I wasn't going to make it easy for him. He was going to have to work very hard to win me over. I needed someone that was going to be all about Kaymee.

Chapter5
Drayton

Kaymee was so beautiful. When my boy Monty asked if I wanted to roll with him to Chicago for the summer, I was down with it. He didn't tell me about meeting anyone until we touched down three days ago. The pictures that he showed me of her didn't do any justice. I usually ended up with the ugly friend. However, she was far from ugly.

She was short about five foot five, thick in all the right places and she was a redbone. I loved a woman with light skin, and the upside of it all, she was a dread head. Her locs were styled nicely and they were red. She had them pulled up in a style that showcased all her facial features. The way her thighs were hugging those shorts made my dick jump, but I knew I needed to calm down.

Hearing all the things that her mom had done and said to her, made me feel sorry for her. But I knew I had to keep her head in the game with some positive words. She still brushed me off, but that would only last a short time. I was determined to get to know her and show her that there was a thing called happiness.

It's been awhile since I looked at a woman in the manner I was seeing Kaymee that day. I believe a big part of it was hearing Poetry say that she had never had sex. The best thing a man could luck up on was a woman that he could teach sexually. Once I kicked her ass in some of these games, she would learn that I wasn't to be fucked with. She was going to be eager to go down to Atlanta to be with me and allow me to love her.

We found a table and looked at the menu to select what we wanted to eat. The waitress came over to see if we were ready to order. The loud chatter of children having fun and adults carrying on conversations filled the building. I hadn't been this excited about being around video games in a very long time.

"Hello, my name is Charlene. I will be your server today. Can I start you guys off with something to drink?" she asked politely.

"I would like a strawberry lemonade, thank you," Kaymee responded.

"I will take a Sprite," Poetry bellowed out.

"Why do you have to be so loud, man," Monty asked, looking at her. We all laughed because she was kind of loud when she said it. "I will take a Pepsi, no ice," he said to the server.

"And I will take a mango smoothie," I said after studying the drink menu.

"Okay, I will bring your drinks right out," she said, walking away after writing our drink orders on her pad.

I looked at Kaymee. She was texting away on her phone. She had a frown on her face that showed that she was irritated. I wasn't the only person that noticed her attitude change. Monty and Poetry also looked at her and the rapid speed of her thumbs as she typed.

"Is everything alright, best friend?" Poetry asked.

She kept texting, then put her phone in her purse. Before she could respond, her phone chimed again. She didn't attempt to retrieve it, she sighed deeply but never lifted her head. The sadness could be seen a mile away. I wanted to gather her in my arms once again, but I didn't want to overstep my boundaries. Poetry must've read my thoughts because she got up and went to her side and hugged her.

"Do we need to take a walk so you can talk about what's going on?" she asked, letting her go.

"Nah, I'm good, boo. I can talk about it right here. I'm done hiding how she treats me. If I continue to bottle this up, I would die a miserable person. That was Dot texting me talking about her money. I told her before I left the house that I would have it for her when I got home. Now she wants it now. I'm not leaving just to take her money that's not even going to make it to the management office. I'm so over all of her bullshit. I can't wait to get away from her."

"What money do you have to give her?" Monty asked.

"I have to pay her three hundred—"

Monty cut her off quickly. "Why are you paying her that kind of money? Y'all stay in the muthafuckin' projects! How the fuck she expect that much from you? That bitch must be out of her damn mind. Fuck her, you are about to have some fun. Don't even think about that shit right now. I don't even want you to answer my question. It's irrelevant," he said, biting his lip. The scowl on his face let me know that he was pissed. I hated when he was upset over me. It was always hard to bring him back down.

"Bro, we are going to enjoy ourselves and forget about Dot's trifling ass. This is not about to spoil the rest of our day," I said, staring in his eyes.

The server came back to the table and I saw Monty's face soften as the minutes went by. She placed our drinks in front of us and took our food orders. The conversation at the table was minimal. The thought of what Kaymee was going through was on my mind heavily. I couldn't take my eyes off her because I was trying to figure out a way to turn that frown into a smile.

"Kaymee, tell me a little bit about yourself," I said lowly.

She didn't say anything right away, so I thought that she was going to just ignore me. Lifting her head, she turned and glanced at me. Her eyes kept shifting nervously as if she didn't know where to begin. I sat quietly, waiting for her to figure it out. I knew she wasn't used to communicating with the opposite sex and I wasn't trying to force anything on her.

"There isn't much to tell about me. I graduated high school a couple weeks ago, top of my class. I work at

Walmart and I can't wait to leave to go to Spelman," she said with a smile.

I could tell that her accomplishments were what made her smile. Her face lit up when she talked about completion of school and her job. I wanted to have her very comfortable with herself by the time she made it to the college life.

I didn't want her to get there and get eaten alive, because it could very well happen. From what I knew at the time, she really hadn't experienced anything in the real world. She had been actually running from her home life and that in itself, could make her a sitting duck.

"That's what's up, shawty. I'm proud of you for completing high school. It's a great feeling when you do your best and end up on top. What do you like to do outside of school and work?" I asked her seriously.

"I really don't do anything other than work and hang with Poetry. I drown myself in my job to avoid going home. I am an only child and my mom doesn't make things very easy for me. I don't want to talk about that right now. It would only make me sad and I'm here to have fun. Oh, here come my buffalo wings. The conversation is over anyway. I'm about to smash!" she said rubbing her hands together.

I couldn't do anything but laugh. She was so cute when she smiled. The dimple on her right cheek was deep. I imagined sticking my tongue in it briefly. The server broke my thoughts when she called out my order. When she placed my cheeseburger and fries in front of me, I didn't waste any time attacking it.

Monty and Poetry were feeding each other fries, looking all in love and shit. My boy loved that girl with all of his heart and he wasn't ashamed to put it on display. When he talked about her, the love spilled out with every word he spoke. Poetry was the same way from what I could tell when they were on video chat. Long distance relationships could be hard, so the trust has to be strong in order for it to work.

Back at school, I didn't have a woman, but I would be the first to say that I had plenty of hoes that I smashed. They didn't mean shit to me. All I needed was to get my dick wet. I never thought about settling down until I laid eyes on Kaymee. I knew I would be able to mold her into the woman that I wanted to spend the rest of my life with. I was willing to wait it out.

"Hey, Dray. What the hell are you over there thinking about?" Monty asked, taking a sip of his drink.

Snapping out of my daydream, I glanced around the table and all eyes were on me. I couldn't even begin to say what the conversation was about. I was so caught up in my thoughts about Kaymee that I tuned everything else out.

"Oh, it was nothing. What were you saying?" I asked, taking a bite of my burger.

"I was asking how much you were going to put on your card for the games. I was gon' go up and load up for everyone."

I turned to sneak a peek at Kaymee and she was back to texting on her phone. I wanted to make sure she had a good time to get her mind off her problems. "We can go up together. I'm finished eating and now it's time to be a kid again. I'm ready to beat some ass in these games," I said, standing from the table.

"Make sure you put enough money on your card because you won't win easily," Poetry said.

Kaymee was digging around in her purse. She got up after pulling out her card. I stared at her for a second before I let the words fall from my lips.

"Where are you going, ma?" I asked.

"I can't play games without coins. I'm going to load my D & B card, too. That's the only way I will be able to have fun along with everyone else," she said with her hands on her hip.

"Nah, that's not about to happen as long as I'm standing here. Let me get your card. I will load it for you. How much were you gonna put on it?" I asked with my hand outstretched.

Kaymee looked at me for what seemed like forever, but it was only about sixty seconds. She finally opened her mouth to answer my question. "I was only putting ten dollars on the card."

I knew then that she had a problem with me added *my* money to her card and threw a low dollar amount at me. I understood where she was coming from and I was going to respect her decision. Nodding my head, I moved away from the table and walked away. Monty caught up to me and slapped me on the back.

"Stop trying so hard, bruh. I can tell that Mee likes you. I want you to understand that she has never had a boyfriend, ever. You are gon' have to take shit slow. She is not like the hoes back at school. You are gonna have to show her that you want to get to know her. I am also hoping if you do break the barrier with my lil' sis, you leave all of those other hoes alone. Kaymee is not one of those girls that deserve to be mistreated. She got enough of that shit going on with her mama," Monty explained.

"I understand what you are saying, fam, and I don't have any intentions of doing her wrong. Poetry let it out the bag that she ain't never fucked before. Shid, she ain't about to give up the ass no time soon. I'm gon' need to keep a bitch or two on the side until she is willing to wet my dick up. I know you look at her as your sister, but you already know that I can't go without sex and she ain't giving up the draws dog."

"The only thing I'm gon' say to you is don't hurt her, Dray. She is as innocent as they come. She is a good girl, man. I introduced you to her because she will be at Spelman and I don't want them thirsty niggas to get a hold of her. You my nigga and I trust that you will do right by her. Don't make me regret giving you the credit and you don't measure up. I won't have a problem fucking you up."

Monty was a man of his word and I knew he meant every word that came out of his mouth. Kaymee meant just as much to him as Poetry did, so I knew I had to play this shit right. We walked to the kiosk and added money onto the cards. Instead of adding ten dollars to Kaymee's card, I put fifty on both of ours. I was ready to show her a good time and money wasn't a problem.

After Monty finished loading his card, we made our way back to the table. The ladies were finishing up the last of their food. I was ready to beat some ass in these games. I walked up to Kaymee and handed her the game card. She took it from my hand, her fingers brushing against mine. The tingling sensation that shot up my arm was one I had never felt for another female.

"Thank you so much for loading my card. I can give you the ten dollars that you put on it," she said, moving her hand back quickly.

"Nah, that's not necessary. Let's go have some fun," I said, looking around the establishment.

I noticed the basketball game was open and I wanted to shoot some hoops. Monty noticed what I was looking at and started laughing. I already knew he was trying to figure out how much he was about to bet. I was ready for his ass, too.

"How much ya puttin' up, homeboy? Twenty?" he asked with a sly grin on his face.

"Shid, whatever. You know how we get down. Let's do it," I said, putting my hand on the small of Kaymee's back, walking toward the game.

This nigga was always willing to lose his money betting on some of everything. He walked behind me, talking more shit than a little bit until we inserted our cards to start the game. The game started and both of us started shooting the balls at the net as soon as they rolled down. Mine were hitting the net with the swish sound with everyone I shot. The girls were cheering us on as we both were trying to win. When the buzzer sounded, Monty won by two points. His ass got lucky.

"Yeah, that's what the fuck I'm talking about! Unass that dub, nigga!" he said, laughing while holding out his hand.

I peeled off a twenty and slapped it in his hand. Kaymee was laughing. I turned to look at her. She was having such a good time and I never wanted to see a frown on her face again. The way her eyes shined when she smiled was a sight to see. I could stand and look at her all day long.

"I want to play one round. Who's gonna play me?" Kaymee asked.

"You know I don't play basketball, bestie. So, it's gonna have to be one of these knuckleheads," Poetry said, pointing between me and Monty.

"I don't have a problem beating a girl. Your money is good for the taking, too," Monty said, laughing.

"Who said I was betting my hard-earned money on a game? Do I look like I have money to lose? You are going to win anyway. I just want to play," Kaymee said with her arms folded.

She looked like a kid that was about to throw a tantrum and it was the cutest thing. Her lips were pouty. I wanted to grab her in my arms and kiss them, but I knew I couldn't. Instead, I spoke up for her, letting her know that I had her back.

"I got forty on Kaymee. I think she is gon' beat the brakes off yo' ass, fam."

"No! I don't want you to bet any money on me. I'm going to lose. I can play basketball, but I don't stand a chance winning against Monty!" she said in a panicky voice.

"Don't worry about it. I have faith in you. All I want you to do is concentrate on your game. Do not look over at his score or what he is doing next to you. Give it your all and let the best man or woman win. Okay?"

"Yo' prep talk ain't gonna stop her from getting that ass whooped, homie. Put ya card in, Mee and let's get this shit over with. Have my green ready, lover boy," Monty said, cackling loudly.

The look that was on Kaymee's face was hilarious. She was really scared. "I want you to relax and concentrate, ma. It's just a game and the money will not make me nor break me. Have fun and whoop his ass," I said, kissing her cheek.

Her face turned bright read instantly, and it made my heart flutter. She squared her shoulders and let out a deep breath. Inserting the card, she waited for the balls to be released. When the balls were free, she grabbed one and shot it.

Swish!

Every damn ball she tossed up hit nothing but net. Her form was on point and she knew to bend at the knees. The way she flicked her wrist was amazing. She was such a girlie girl that one wouldn't have thought she would know how to handle a   basketball. The clock was winding down and there were ten seconds left on the clock. Her eyes never left the rim and her hands kept a ball in it at all times. When the buzzer sounded, Monty had seventy points, but Kaymee had seventy-eight points.

"That's my best friend, that's my best friend!" Poetry sang dance around Monty.

I scooped her up in my arms and swung her around. She beat that nigga at his own game. I put her down on her feet and pointed at the score. "Look at that shit, shawty. You beat his ass by eight points. You have earned bragging rights!" I said, give her high five.

"That's bullshit! This machine is broken! Where is management? I need to report a machine that has malfunctioned." Monty yelled, looking around.

"Malfunctioned my ass, brah. Give me my schmoney, nigga." Kaymee said with her hand held out.

"I'm not giving you nothing until they come and check this damn machine. Obviously, this muthafucka is broken. There's no way you just beat me, and by eight points! Nah, I'm not letting this ride." He said shaking his head continuously.

One of the attendants came over to check the machine. After he was finished, it was confirmed the score tallied correctly, so Monty lost fair and square. Even though there wasn't anything wrong with the machine, he still insisted that the machine wasn't working.

"That machine has to be broken! It wasn't giving me my points. They must've went to her score instead of mine! I want my muthafuckin' money back!" Monty was screaming at the young attendant who looked like he was about to cry.

"Bae, stop being a sore loser and give my girl her damn money. There are plenty more games here for us to play and there will be no more betting. We are here to have fun," Poetry said to Monty.

"Poetry, I'm not paying because the game wasn't working."

"If you don't hand over that money, you will spend the remainder of the summer stroking your dick," she said, walking off.

Monty stood, watching Poetry walk away through the crowd of kids. He hurriedly went into his pocket and handed Kaymee two twenties. Both Kaymee and I laughed hard because this fool was threatened by Poetry, complying fast. He kept looking around, trying to figure out where she went.

"Man, I have to go find her. I will let her know that I was only joking. The last thing I need is my baby holding out on the gushy. I love her too much and if she cuts me off in the bedroom, there ain't no telling what I would do," he said in a rush.

The way he hurried off into the crowd was funny because he looked like a little kid that was lost. Once Monty was out of sight, I got lost in Kaymee's eyes. She had the most beautiful brown eyes I've ever seen. I wanted to kiss her on her full pouty lips, but I didn't know how she would react to it. Instead, I grabbed her hand and led her to the other side of the building. I was surprised she didn't pull away. That was the second time she allowed me to touch her.

We played game after game until about ten o'clock that night. Monty and Poetry walked over to us while we were racing on motorcycles. Kaymee was killing me and I was enjoying every minute of it. The race was over and Kaymee was the winner. She had been kicking my ass all day. She didn't lie when she said she was ready to be competitive. I loved a woman that loved some of the same things I did.

I learned that she was a diehard *Chicago Cubs* fan. I've never met a woman that watched baseball. That was like sitting and watching paint dry on a wall. She also loved basketball, football, and hockey. I was with her until she said hockey. I wasn't watching that shit for anybody. But I was ready to talk mad shit with her about basketball. I loved the *Cleveland Cavaliers*, but she didn't care for LeBron. I knew the tension would be high when we watched the games together.

"I'm tired of whooping on your ass, Dray. Let's call it a night. I'm tired and I still have to stop at the bank to get this money for the evil lady," she said, climbing off the motorcycle.

When she swung her leg over the seat, my mouth watered instantly. The way her shorts rose under her ass cheeks was picture perfect. She was thicker than a snicker and I couldn't wait to claim all of her. Yeah, she was definitely worth waiting on.

"I had a good time today. Maybe we can do it again sometime. You are one cool chick."

"Thank you. I had fun today, too. I enjoyed your company and I would like to hang out with you again," she smiled.

I was glad to hear her say that she would like to see me again. I had to try hard to suppress the joy that I was feeling on the inside. I had plans to treat this girl the way she was supposed to be treated. I wanted her beautiful smile to stay on her face at all times and I wanted to be the reason it was there to stay.

Chapter 6
Kaymee

That day was the first time that I enjoyed myself in the presence of a boy. Well, in Dray's case, a man. I liked him because he was fun to kick it with. He kept my mind off what awaited me at home. When we left Dave and Busters, Monty refused to take me to the bank to get Dot's money. I was nervous about going home without it because I knew she was going to try to fight me.

It was almost midnight when we finally headed to my neighborhood. Monty had given Dray his cut of the money they had won playing basketball earlier. I sat quietly in the back seat of the car, thinking about the bullshit that my mama was about to be on. I had fun with my friends but my mood went from glorious to sad the closer I got home.

I didn't say anything to Dray the entire ride. He kept stealing looks at me, but he never said anything. As Monty pulled up to my building, I sat staring out the window taking in the scenery. There were guys standing in front of the building. I was tired of having to pass by them just to get into my apartment.

This neighborhood could make anyone depressed just by looking at what went on every day. I was bigger than this place and I had plans of getting out. I had to break the chain that tried to stifle me all my life.

"Mee, are you okay?" Monty asked.

I nodded my head and reached for the door to get out. Stalling for a minute, I sighed long and hard opening the door. I got out and went to the front passenger window, giving Poetry a hug.

"I'll talk to you tomorrow, bestie. Don't do nothing I wouldn't do," I whispered in her ear.

"You already know that I have to take my ass home. I'm already late for curfew. Ain't nothing happening," she shot back.

"I'll be right back. I'm gonna walk sis upstairs," Monty said to Poetry.

He opened the door to get out and I walked in front of the car. Dray got out and stepped in front of me. He stood staring at me for a few minutes, then he hugged me tightly. I felt his hand move to my ass. I tried to step out of his grasp but he wouldn't let me go.

"I know you will be in there fighting yo' mama if you go in there without any money. I don't need yo' pretty ass whoopin' her ass, so you got five hunnid in yo' pocket. Keep the change. It's my thanks to you for showing me a good time today. I look forward to seeing you later," Dray said lowly in my ear.

"Dray, I can't let you do that," I said, trying to break the hold he had on me for the second time. He wasn't trying to hear anything I was saying. "I have the money and she will get it tomorrow when I go to the ATM. That is a lot of money you just gave me and I can't accept it. No one is giving that kind of money without wanting something in return."

He released me and placed his hands on my shoulders. "Let me explain something to you, love. I'm not the nigga that does anything for a woman and looks for something in return. I gave you that bread because I wanted you to have it, no strings attached. The only thing I want you to do is keep rising to the top. Don't let your moms continue to beat your self-esteem into the ground and stay beautiful. The things I mentioned, you were already doing before you met me. Keep it going," he said, kissing my forehead.

"Thank you so much," I said, turning to walk away.

"Aye, Kaymee!" he yelled out to me. I turned back around to face him and he walked over to me. "Gimme yo' phone."

I took my phone out and pressed the button to unlock it before handing it to him. He pressed a couple of buttons and handed the phone back to me. I heard a sound come from his phone as he took it off of his hip. He looked down and pressed a series of buttons, putting it back in place.

"I have you locked in. I'll be talking to you soon, cutie. Goodnight," he said, walking back to the car.

Watching him get back in the car, I headed up the walkway where Monty was waiting. I couldn't hide the smile that appeared on my face. Monty started laughing, shaking his head when I got close enough to him. I didn't know what he was laughing about, but at that point, I didn't care. I just wanted to get in the house and go to bed.

"I see you a little smitten with my boy," he said cockily. "You can thank me in the morning," he said, punching my arm playfully

"Shut up, nigga! He is nice and I can see myself falling for him, but I want to take things slow. I don't know anything about having a boyfriend, so I want us to become friends first. You of all people know that my schooling comes before everything. I'm not ready for the drama of being someone's girlfriend."

"I hear ya, sis. Take it as slow as you need to. Don't ever allow anyone to pressure you into doing something you are not ready for. You set the tone and stick to what you say. If you want to be with him after a while, do that shit. But if you decide he's not for you, then walk away from that shit. It's that simple."

We were almost to the building's entrance when someone hollered out, "What up, Kaymee? Who is this nigga walking up in my shit?"

I knew it was the dude from earlier that tried to talk to me. He really thought this building belonged to him. It was kind of dark out front, so Monty's face couldn't really be seen. I didn't respond to the question. Instead, I continued walking towards the building.

"I know you hear me talking to yo' ass, Kaymee. Don't get dude fucked up! You know we don't do new muthafuckas around here," he said, walking quickly in front of us.

The last thing I wanted was for this nigga to get in Monty's face. If he knew what was good for him, he would back the fuck up. This was not what he wanted. This would be the time that he decided what battle he wanted to tackle.

"Okay, since she don't' want to tell you that you can't go in my building, I will. Yo' ass can't go in that bitch, nigga."

Monty pushed me behind him and stood toe to toe with the dude. Next thing I knew, he started laughing at him. I didn't know what he found amusing, but I was curious to find out. The dude didn't appreciate Monty laughing in his face. His nose started flaring in and out rapidly, but he didn't stand down.

"See, lil nigga. I should slap the fuck out of you for being so muthafuckin' stupid. You should know who the fuck you steppin' to before you do it. I used to change yo' fuckin' pampers when ya strung out ass mama wouldn't. I was the reason yo' lil ass had food in your stomach, a roof over yo' head, and clothes on ya muthafuckin' back."

Monty stepped into the light and the dude's eyes got big as saucers. He couldn't find his voice once he saw who he was talking reckless to. Monty grabbed him by his collar damn near choking him. His shirt was so tight around his neck that he was struggling to move. Every time he tried pulling away, he only caused the material to cut deeper into his neck.

"Deshaun Harris, don't fuckin' play with me. I guess somebody gave yo' ass a spot and you think you're bad. What they should've taught you was how to move in silence, my nigga. You got one more time to disrespect that one," he said, pointing his thumb behind him at me. "I'll kill you myself, bitch. I don't give a fuck what you got going on out here. You will respect me," he snarled in his face.

"My bad, my bad, Monty. I didn't know that was you, fam. I didn't mean nothing by it. I swear I didn't. You know I would never disrespect you, but I think you should let me go because you are making me look like a bitch out here," he said lowly.

"I don't give a fuck who's watching! If you gon' be about this life, you have to be in character at all times. Never let anyone, including me, punk yo' lil ass on your own turf. I'll be here for a couple months. You know where I'm at. Come see me so I can school your dumb ass before you die out here trying to be hard. While yo' ass standing around doing nothing, you will make sure nothing happens to her," he said, pointing his thumb over his shoulder at me a second time. "If anything happens to her, I want you to call me ASAP! Is that understood?"

Deshaun shook his head up and down and Monty pushed him back a few steps. He straightened out his shirt and grabbed his phone out of his pocket. "What's your number, fam?" he asked, looking around at his boys.

Monty snatched the phone and entered his number, giving it back after he was done. "Remember what I said, youngin'. Don't let me have to repeat myself. Pull yo' muthafuckin' pants up, too. How the fuck you gon' protect ya'self when yo' strap is in your pocket and your pocket is at yo' damn knees? Yeah, come see me, lil' dummy. Let's go. Mee," he said, walking away shaking his head.

We were walking to the entrance and one of the guys that was standing by the door looked Monty up and down. Monty wasn't paying him any attention, but I saw him taking small steps with one hand at his side. I glanced down and saw he had pulled his gun. Before I could say anything, Deshaun ran up to the guy and whispered something in his ear. The expression that was displayed on his face told me that Monty was well known far more than I knew.

***

The elevator still wasn't working and I hated walking up the stairs. Going down wasn't a problem. That was the easy part. Walking up six flights of stairs is what killed you. I got to the door and turned to bid Monty goodnight. I wanted to tell him what the dude downstairs did, but I knew he would beat his ass as soon as he saw him. I didn't want him getting in any trouble, so I kept my mouth closed.

"Thank you for walking me to the door, bro. Be careful when you get back downstairs. I will call you tomorrow," I said, giving him a hug.

"You don't have to thank me for doing anything for you, Mee. I will always be here when you need me. I want you to go straight to your room when you go inside. I don't want to have to come back over here tonight. If I do, yo' mama getting fucked up and that's on everything I love. Don't say shit to her, Kaymee. Keep your cool. Call me if you need me," he said, pulling back from me.

"I will," I said as I knocked on the door.

I had to knock three times before I heard Dot shuffling to the door. She stood there for about three minutes before she opened it. She had on her raggedy blue robe, dirty house shoes, and her hair was all over her head. The smell of alcohol hit me in the face the minute she opened the door. I knew then I wasn't going to sleep any time soon.

"Why are you knocking on my door at this time of the night, bitch?" She didn't see Monty standing off to the side, so she continued to talk shit. "Do you have my muthafuckin' money?" she asked, rolling her eyes. Before I could answer, she started yapping again. "If not, you can go find somewhere to lay your head until you get it. I wouldn't give a damn if you slept on a park bench," she said with her hand resting on the knob.

The movement that Monty made when she said that caused me to jump. He was in her face immediately and whatever she was about to say was cut short. Her mouth was stuck in an "O" shape, her eyes bucked big as hell. She stepped back a little bit, putting space between Monty and herself. She knew he didn't play any games when it came to me.

"How about you let her in the damn house and leave her the fuck alone. I can't believe that you are threatening your teenage daughter with sleeping outside because she don't have the money for your rent! Get yo' dried up ass out and get a fuckin' job! Or how about you tell one of those hoe ass niggas that's always laying in ya bed, waiting to get his dick sucked to pay that shit. I can't stand yo' good for nothing ass, bitch! If I find out that you in this muthafucka calling her anything other than the name you gave her, I'm gon' beat yo' ass."

I didn't know what was in store for me after that, but Dot stepped to the side, allowing me access to enter. Looking back at Monty, his eyes still burned a hole through the side of her face. "Call me if you need to, Mee. I don't give a fuck what time it is either, because I will be back," he said, walking off after throwing another sinister look Dot's way.

Going through the door, I felt the tension inside of the apartment and boy was it thick. I tried to go to my room without saying anything to Dot, but she wanted to argue. Knowing that Monty was gone, I was scared as hell. Deep inside, I knew what Dot was about personally. He only knew what I told him. That night, I wished I never told him what happened.

"Bitch, you out there telling muthafuckas my business, now? Who the fuck do he think he is, coming at me about my child? There is nothing his ass can do to me! I would have someone shoot his ass in the fuckin' face coming at me like he did!" she screamed at my back.

I continued to my room without saying anything to her. I was not in the mood to go through this shit with her. She was only going to come in my room and turn into the bully that she was, blaming me for everything that had taken place. Yes, I told what was going on with me at home. Did I regret it? In a way I did, but that didn't mean she should come to me throwing it in my face. What's right is right and what's wrong is wrong, and she was wrong as hell.

The sound of her house shoes sliding along the floor let me know that she was quickly moving in my direction. I was in my room taking off my sandals when she stormed in. I tried my best to ignore her because I didn't want the conflict. That didn't mean anything because obviously she did.

I removed the sandal from my left foot when I felt the first blow on the left side of my head. My teeth clattered together and I bit my tongue. It felt like she hit me with a brick. I automatically balled up on my bed, holding my head. My mouth filled with blood as I swallowed the metallic tasting fluid. I could feel my tongue swelling and my head was throbbing.

"Bitch, I don't know what possessed you to go outside of this house telling any damn body what the fuck I do! I'm gonna teach your ass once and for all. What happens in my house, stays in my muthafuckin' house!"

I didn't hear when she walked over to my bed, so that only meant she took off her shoes. I was having a hard time seeing because my vision was blurred. When she grabbed me by my hair and slung me on the floor, my face hit the corner of the dresser. I had never had a fight in my life and the first one was with my mama. I was defenseless because she caught me off guard and I couldn't regroup.

"Bitch, you are gonna learn to stop bringing outside muthafuckas into family affairs," she screamed, kicking me in my side repeatedly.

The pain that shot through my body was unbearable. I curled up in a ball, but it didn't help. The tears rolled down my face continuously. I didn't have the strength to wipe them away. I looked up to see where she was and I saw her foot about to come down on my head. Finding the energy, I grabbed her foot causing her to fall to the floor. I rolled over while she was trying to get up. I stood up at the same time she did. Knowing that she was going to beat my ass, I wasn't about to go out without a fight.

My head was hurting badly. The pain was excruciating. I didn't know how much longer I was going to last without falling out. The rage in Dot's eyes held the look of hate. In my mind, I knew that she saw me as one of the bitches on the street. She was not going to show me any mercy, and I wasn't about to stand there and let her beat me without fighting back.

"Oh, so you think you can take me on, bitch? I'm gonna show your ass that I'm not to be fucked with. You will learn to do what the fuck I say, not what the hell you want to do. Bitch, I have been the muthafucka taking care of yo' ass when yo' no good ass daddy decided he didn't want to be with me no more. I didn't sign up for this shit. He played a part in this shit, too!" she said, punching me in my mouth.

She let the cat out the bag. The man that I had never met a day in my life was the reason I was being treated like yesterday's trash. That shit didn't have a muthafuckin' thing to do with me. I didn't ask to be brought into this fucked up world. Her ass should've swallowed my ass if she didn't want a fuckin' kid.

"Ohhhh, so the truth comes out," I said, spitting blood on the floor. "You couldn't love me because a nigga didn't love you enough to stay with you? I told you I would find out the reason you hated me so much. So, I'm paying for something that I had no control over. Yeah, you are a pitiful muthafucka! I don't have no respect for you, man. You want to fight, let's get this shit out of the way then. This will be the last time you put your fuckin' hands on me. I was never your child, I was my daddy's child. Act like you don't know me, hoe!"

I didn't know where that boost of courage came from, but I knew she had pissed me off. At that moment, I didn't feel an ounce of pain. I had been trying to be the best child I could all my life. I begged and pleaded for this muthafucka to love me, but she couldn't because I probably was a splitting image of my daddy. Why take that shit out on me, though? I won't know the answer to that question because from this point on, I didn't give a fuck.

Charging towards her, I hit her in her face repeatedly and didn't stop. She was more experienced at fighting than I was, so she took the punches that I threw at her. She grabbed me by my locs, delivering hit after hit to my face. I tried to swing back, but it was no use. She was whooping my ass, slinging me around like a rag doll.

"This is how I beat a bitch in the street. You wanted it, so I'm giving it to your ass! That will be the last time you disrespect me!"

She was beating my ass and I knew with every punch, she saw my daddy.

"Arrrrgggggghhh!" I screamed when she hit me in my eye. It felt like my eye was pushed to the back of my head. I landed on the floor, falling next to my baseball bat that was in the corner. I couldn't see out of my right eye but I could see that bat clear as day with the left one. I didn't want to hit her with it but that was the only way to get her off me. Grabbing the bat, I shoved the handle into her stomach.

She groaned when I made contact with the bat. Raising the bat over my head, I swung at her head. I closed my eyes not wanting to want to see what would come from the impact. The bat was snatched from my hands as I was pushed onto my bed. I struggled to get up, turning around I was eye to eye with one of Dot's boyfriends. This one was actually cool. His name was Damon. He was the only one that told Dot when she was in the wrong.

"What the fuck is wrong with, Dot? I know muthafuckin' well you ain't in here beating this girl like this! Look at her muthafuckin' face!" he screamed at her.

"Don't come in here taking up for this bitch! She wanted to be treated like a hoe on the street, so I gave her what the fuck she asked for. You can't tell me how to discipline her ass! She is gonna learn that I don't take disrespect too well. Fuck her, Dame. I'll kill this lil' bitch!" she said, charging at me.

Damon pushed her back and she hit the wall. "You are out of your fuckin' mind, Dot! I've never seen this girl do nothing wrong! You always find a reason to be mad at her and I'm tired of this shit. Get your ass in there and put on some clothes so we can take her to the fuckin' hospital!" he growled at her.

"I'm not taking her ass no muthafuckin' where! If she needs to go, she will take herself. I don't give a fuck about her. While she's out there, she needs to suck a dick or two and get my money," she snarled and limped out of my room.

I cried so hard, the tears burned the eye she had hit me in. I pushed myself off the bed and limped towards the door.

"Kaymee, come on so I can take you to the hospital," Damon said softly.

I really didn't want to go to the hospital because deep down, I didn't want Dot to get in trouble for what she did to me. Still, I knew that I had to go to make sure everything was all right. I looked in the mirror and the reflection that stared back at me was of one that I didn't recognize.

Dot had beat me so bad, both of my eyes were swollen and one was beet red. The left side of my face was swollen as well as my lips. My side was aching with every move that I made. The shit hurt with every breath I took. The tears that ran down my face only made the pain worse. My heart was aching because I'd never thought my mother would go to this extreme all because my daddy left her.

Chapter 7
Dot

Kaymee really pissed me off with her shit. After she was out ignoring my calls and text messages as I tried to figure out where the hell my money was, here she was now getting flipped at the mouth like I was one of her little friends or something.

I couldn't wait for her uppity ass to get out of my damn house. I didn't know where the hell she got her attitude from, but I knew that I was going to correct it when she came home.

She had already disrespected me before she left earlier and I wasn't going to let her think it was okay to continue that shit. When I got pregnant with her, I was happy and couldn't wait to bring a child in the world. I had the perfect relationship and I knew I would be the best mother to my child.

Jonathan and I had been together since we were fifteen years old. I had been careful every time we had sex. He was my first everything. One night we went to a concert and we had a lot to drink. I had a fake ID, but he didn't need one because he looked older than his seventeen years. That night we were on some spontaneous type shit. We ended up fucking in his car right in the parking lot of the United Center.

Jonathan was sucking on my left nipple, while grinding his dick into my center. The friction from his jeans was hitting my clit just right and my kitty loved the way he had her feeling. I wasn't trying to dry hump any longer, so I reached down and unfastened his pants.

"I need you inside of me, Jon," I moaned, wrapping my hand around his pole. I started stroking it up and down until he started pumping my hand. I knew if I allowed him to enjoy the hand job that I gave too much, he was going to

cum. My lower lips were aching to be touched and he was about to do just that.

The skirt that I had on was way above my waist and the thong that I had on wasn't in the way at all. I rubbed his lil' man against my clit and damn near went crazy. My tunnel was wet, just the way he liked it. I guided him into my tight hole and he clamped down on my nipple.

"Oh shit, girl!" he groaned in my ear. "Sssssss, this pussy feels so good, ma."

He threw my leg over the headrest and the other damn near in the back window. I was spread eagle and he was balls deep inside of me. Jonathan was beating my cat up like he had something to prove and I was milking him for all he had.

"Turn that ass over, baby. I want to get all in them guts," he said, smacking my thigh.

I placed one of my feet on the floor of the car and kneeled on my left knee. Jonathan grabbed me around my waist with one hand and shoved his member inside with the other. He smacked me on my ass and it hurt so good. With every thrust, my head it the window. It was so hot in that car the windows were fogged to the max.

"Yes, right there, baby. Fuck me harder!" I moaned, willingly throwing my ass back on him.

Putting both of my hands against the window to balance myself, I felt him slip his thumb in my ass. When he did that, the devil himself appeared in the car. I had an outer body experience because he had never done that before. The feeling was sensational. I started cumming all over his seats.

"Shit! That pussy gripping my dick, baby. Throw that ass back!" he growled in my ear.

He took his thumb out of my ass and replaced it with his dick. I instantly deflated. The pain that I felt was indescribable. "Please take it out! It hurt so bad, Jon! It hurts!" I cried out to him.

"Baby, you have to relax, it will only hurt for a little while then you will really enjoy it," he said.

I didn't know how he thought relaxing was going to ease the pain that I was feeling. How about he let me stick something in his ass and see if he could relax. I relaxed my entire body and let him have his way with my backdoor. He started stroking slowly and I was still tensed, there was no getting through this pain. The tears were streaming down my face and I didn't let him know, my focus was on pleasing my man.

He reached down and started rubbing my clit with a vengeance, pumping at the same time. I didn't know why he didn't do that in the first place. My kitty started singing like a canary. My attention was on getting the nut forming in my stomach. I forgot which hole he was in. I started backing my ass up, meeting him thrust for thrust.

"Aaaaaargh! This is the best feeling in the world, Dee!" He stroked a couple more times and snatched his dick out, putting it in my kitty.

The rhythm we had going synchronized perfectly. When he pinched my nipple, my walls closed around him tightly and my cup overflowed. "Yes, baby. I'm cumming!" I screamed out in ecstasy throwing my head back.

"I'm right there with you!" He hit my kitty a good three times, tightening his grip on my waist. I felt all his babies let loose in my tunnel. "Grrrrrrrrr! Oh yeah!" he growled loudly. I reached between my legs and massage his balls gently, while continuing to move. I wanted him to be satisfied completely from that session. He fell onto my back breathing hard.

"Thank you, baby. That was the best one yet. If you keep taking care of me like that, I'll marry you, girl," he said, kissing my cheek.

We cleaned up with the wet wipes that I kept in my purse. Finding our clothes, we rushed to get dressed so we could get out of the parking lot. Jonathan got out of the car and hopped into the driver's seat. I climbed my ass through the seats and got comfortable in the passenger's seat.

Jonathan kept looking at me smiling and I blushed. Sex always brought us closer together and I loved him so much. He was driving slowly as hell but at least we weren't arguing. I turned on the radio and the sultry sound of Anita Baker flowed out of the speakers. Good love had me thinking about the time we spent together and the future ahead.

Pregnancy was the last thought on my mind, but I started feeling sick constantly weeks after the concert. I was taking everything under the sun to feel better because I hated going to the hospital. Thinking I had the flu, I went to the clinic probably a month later to see what was going on. The doctor insisted I take a pregnancy test and I obliged once he confirmed that I didn't have the flu. When the results came back positive, I was ecstatic. I couldn't wait to tell Jonathan.

I went home and called him immediately. He answered on the second ring, sounding happy to hear from me. "Hey, baby!" I sang into the phone.

"What got you in such a happy mood today?" he asked.

I didn't want to tell him the news over the phone, so I buttered him up a little bit. "You have me in the mood that I'm in. This is the first time I've spoken to you all day and I've missed you. Can you come see me for a little while?"

I was praying he said yes because I didn't know how long I would be able to keep this a secret.

"Yeah, I'll be there in five minutes. I'm already around the corner from your house. I'm at the park."

"Okay, well I'm about to walk over there then. I need to get some air anyway."

"That's cool. I'm walking to meet you, so come on," he said, hanging up.

Slipping my feet in my shoes, I left out of my apartment to go deliver the news to Jonathan. By the time I made my *way out of the building, he was standing at the end of the walkway waiting on me. He was dressed in black basketball shorts with a black tank top on, showing off the many tats he had on his arms.*

"What's going on, Dee?" he said as I ran into his arms.

"I have something to tell you and I didn't want to tell you over the phone. I wanted to see your reaction for myself. I know you are going to be just as excited as I am," I said with a big smile on my face. "Jon, we are having a baby!" I said, jumping up and down.

"Ain't shit happy about that, Dot!" he yelled, running his hand down his face.

I knew he was pissed when he used the name that everybody else used when they addressed me. Jonathan was the only person that called me Dee. My smile fell immediately from my face. I didn't understand why he was upset. We'd been together for two years and he always talked about how much he loved me.

"You gotta get an abortion, yo'. I'm seventeen years old and you are, too. We ain't ready for a damn baby. My mama would kill me! I will pay for the shit. We can go to the clinic tomorrow. There's no way you can have that baby."

When he uttered those words, my heart broke into a million pieces. I started to cry, preventing me from saying anything. I couldn't find my voice. Taking a deep breath after a couple seconds, I finally found the words to say to him.

"How dare you tell me to kill my baby! Both of us knew the consequences of unprotected sex. I didn't make and create this baby alone, Jonathan. You played a major part. I will not raise this baby alone!" I yelled, poking him in the chest.

"You won't have to take care of the baby alone because there won't be a baby! Now, when the fuck do you want to go to the abortion clinic, Dot?" he asked angrily.

I wasn't trying to hear none of the shit that he was saying. He had to be a damn fool if he thought I was getting rid of my baby. This baby was made out of love and he was going to love us both. He was crazy as hell if he thought I was giving him a date and time to get an abortion, it wasn't happening.

"Jonathan, I will not be going to anybody's clinic. Not today, tomorrow, or the next day. In seven months, this baby will enter the world healthy. No one would be able to convince me to do otherwise, so get ready to be a daddy, nigga," I said with a smirk on my face.

"If you think a baby is gon' make me happy, you are wrong as fuck. That damn baby just broke us up. Don't call me until you are ready to go to the clinic. I've already told you that I wasn't ready to have a baby!" he said, turning to walk down the street.

"You ain't ready to take care of a baby but you were damn sure ready every time you wanted to practice! You ain't shit, Jonathan. Wait until I tell yo' mama about this shit, punk ass nigga."

I was yelling at his back because he never stopped walking. He threw his arms up a couple times before I saw him pull out his phone. I knew he was calling his petty ass mama before I did. The bitch didn't like me anyway.

He ended up leaving Chicago, moving away to live with his grandmother. I didn't know what state he moved to either. It was like he fell off the face of the earth. He left me to tell my mother I was pregnant on my own and that the daddy left me high and dry. I didn't tell her until I was four months and that was only because she caught me without my baggy clothes on.

I was sitting on my bed reading a baby book. My ear buds were in my ear and the music was extra loud. I didn't even know she had walked into my room. That's just how engulfed I was in reading that book. Everything happened so fast. My mama snatched the ear bud out of my ear and started going in on my ass.

"I know muthafuckin' well you are about to tell me you have a tumor." My mama was calm as fuck and I was stuck on stupid. I didn't know what to say. She'd caught me by surprise. "Your lil' fast ass done went and got yourself knocked up! Who is the damn daddy, huh?"

"Jonathan is the father of my baby, ma. There hasn't been anyone else in my life except him. I don't know why you think I'm out there being a hoe or something. I've only had one boyfriend and that's Jonathan!"

I was so mad that she thought I was sleeping with more than one person. I had never been the kind of girl to sleep around. I knew she was upset but damn, give me some kind of credit.

"Where the hell is he because I haven't seen him in months? Let me take a guess. He left your ass high and dry to deal with this shit alone after you told him you were pregnant or was it him that suggested an abortion because he didn't want a kid? Which one was it?"

She was no longer calm about the situation. My mama was downright pissed. I couldn't even look her in the face because she hit everything head-on. I was so embarrassed, not wanting her to know that she was absolutely correct about everything she said.

"I don't know where Jonathan is. He hasn't answered any of my messages or calls since the day I told him that I was pregnant. The very words that you threw at me, he did too. I don't know what I'm going to do. I didn't tell you I was having a baby because I knew that Jonathan and I could raise this baby together. He will be back. I know he won't leave me like this," I cried.

"All I have to say is this. You made your bed, now you gotta lay in it. Jonathan is a coward for running away from his responsibilities. He's not coming back, so you can stop with that one. That's something you should've thought about before you decided to hide a baby. I bet you thought having this baby was going to make him stay with you, huh? You should've came and talked to me! I would've told you dumb ass that a baby wouldn't make a muthafucka stay with you. I bet your stupid ass don't even know his social security number or his last name for that matter! I hate to say this shit, but you cannot stay in my house with a baby. I have five other kids to take care of and there's no room for another little person."

When she said that I had to get out of her house, I was shocked. I didn't think in a million years my mama would turn her back on me, but that's exactly what she was doing. The tears flowed continuously down my face. I couldn't do anything but shake my head at her.

"So, you are putting me out on the street with a baby? What happened to moral support? What happened to talking to me about what I would expect when I have this baby? What about gathering me in your arms and telling me everything would be alright?"

"Oh, I will support your decision. I'm going to do it from afar. I will help you with this baby by making sure you have your own place to lay your head. After that, you're on your own. I will help with the baby when I decide to help. I will not raise this baby for you. That will be your job. You wanted to be grown, here's your chance. Be ready to go to the management office in an hour. I have some calls to make," she said, walking out of my room.

Dragging me down to the management office of the projects that we lived in, she asked the manager if there were any vacancies. She was a friend of the manager, telling her to fill out the application. She even agreed to put it at the top of the list. I wasn't ready to be on my own, but my mama wasn't trying to help me beyond this point.

In my mind, Jonathan was coming back and we were going to be happy as a family. I realized that he wasn't coming back when after a while. I was six months pregnant and he still hadn't returned. He changed his number after a while and his mama told me I wasn't welcomed at her house. To make matters worse, my mama had basically disowned me.

I fell into a deep depression and dropped out of school. I moved into my apartment when I was eight months along. I applied for government assistance and Section Eight to help me pay my bills. I was granted everything I applied for, so that was all I needed to survive. I wasn't trying to work for anyone when I had a guaranteed check coming in every month.

I delivered my baby girl July 11, 1992 at five forty-three in the morning. She was five pounds, seven ounces, and seventeen inches long. I named her Kaymee only because the nurse suggested it. I didn't give a fuck what her name was. When the nurse placed her in my arms, I immediately gave her back, telling her that I was in too much pain to hold her. The lil' bitch looked just like Jonathan and it hurt to look at her.

From that day forward, I didn't like the lil' girl. I didn't want anything to do with her. Even though my mama said she wasn't raising my child, she did. That girl spent majority of her life at my mama's house.

I was running the streets doing what I wanted to do. In my mind, I didn't have a baby. She belonged to my mama. When she would come home with me, I didn't pay her any attention. My girlfriends bought here whatever she needed, leaving my money for me.

I got the lil' bitch back fulltime when my mama passed away in nineteen ninety-eight. I cried more about raising my own child than the fact that my mama had died. I knew I wasn't going to do right by her because I had shit to do in the streets.

When I found out Jonathan was sending my mama money for the lil bitch every month, I made sure to forward all her mail to my address. That was more money for me. I was pissed because my mama never told me shit about it. I couldn't confront her ass because she was dead and gone.

My mama taught her most of what she knew and I was delighted because I didn't have to do much. Yeah, she was six years old, but the way she took care of herself, I couldn't tell. That's why I didn't hesitate to leave her alone to do me.

Her ass was so much like that lil' girl from the movie *Matilda,* too damn smart if you asked me. Once she showed me she was capable of fending for herself, she was on her own. As long as no one called the people on my ass, I was good. I laid down law and told her what she could and couldn't do and she followed the rules.

When she graduated high school, that was when she decided it was time to speak her fuckin' mind. Her mouth was so flip that I found myself wanting to slap the shit out of her more every day. Don't get it twisted, I whooped her ass before then, but the night she showed her ass with that nigga Monty was the first time I took it to that extreme. She brought that shit on herself.

I tried to knock her fuckin' head off. She wanted to be Billy Bad Ass and I let her ass have it. I didn't know who she thought she was talking to, but whatever happened in my house should've never made its way outside my door.

I didn't know how bad I had beat her ass, but it pissed me off when Dame came in trying to save her muthafuckin' ass. All I knew was I wasn't taking her no damn where. If he wanted to take her to the hospital, he could be my guest because I wasn't going.

After they left, I got in the tub because my body was aching. I relaxed, thinking about everything that had transpired. Once I did, the shit only made me mad all over again. The fucked up part about all of this was the fact that I really didn't have a reason to be mad at her.

I didn't feel bad about what I had done. I beat her ass for the disrespect from earlier, as well. How the hell did she think she was going to get away with questioning me like she was the mother and I was the child?

After getting out of the tub, I went into my bedroom and laid across the bed and started watching TV. I didn't know what time I dozed off. I heard the front door open then closed. At that point, I glanced at the clock. It read six thirty in the morning.

There was a lot of shuffling around going on that made me get up to see what it was. I went to the bitch's room and saw Dame helping her into her bed. It pissed me off because he was handling her like her ass was fragile.

"When you finish playing Nurse Betty, you can get the fuck out of my house," I said, walking out of the doorway.

Five minutes later, Dame stood and leaned against my door and stared at me. I ignored his ass until he opened his mouth talking crazy. "Dot, you're not gonna ask about yo' fuckin' daughter?"

I turned around to face him with a frown plastered on my face. This muthafucka needed to get out of my house talking that bullshit. Didn't he know that I didn't give a fuck about that bitch that was lying in the other room? Obviously not, as he stood there waiting on a reply that he was not about to receive.

"You broke three of her fuckin' ribs, Dot! She has a blood clot in her eye! There's a hole in her tongue because her teeth went through it from a punch you sent to her damn mouth! Did you see the bruises on her face, Dot? On top of that, she has a mild concussion! Do you even care? She didn't even tell them that you did this shit to her and she begged me not to tell either! But I wish I would've said something because you have no fuckin' remorse for what you have done!" he screamed, stomping over to where I was laying.

"That was her fault! She shouldn't have come at me like she was about that life. Tell that lil' bitch to stay in her fuckin' lane. I'll do the shit all over again if she decides to tell my business again. I wish somebody would show up at my house over this shit. Now, show yo'self out of my fuckin' house and leave the key on the dresser. I don't need yo' ass no more," I said, turning over to continue watching TV.

"Change the locks, hoe. I'm not leaving this key because I may need to come back to save her life. I've never seen a grown ass woman that was jealous of a damn child, your own child at that! You are gonna meet that bitch name Karma and she is gonna beat the fuck out of you. Don't call me for shit, but if Kaymee calls me and say you looked at her wrong, I'm gonna kill you hoe," he said, walking away from my room.

I heard my front door slam and I shook my head, lying down to finally go to sleep. I wasn't worried about Dame. That lil' bitch, or anyone else for that matter. Everybody better stay the fuck away from me with the dumb shit. I thought to myself, closing my eyes.

Chapter 8
Poetry

Monty told me that he had to put Dot in her place the night we went out. When he came back to the car, he had smoke coming out of his ears. He was mad as hell. At first, he wouldn't say anything, but eventually he told Dray and I what happened after he smoked a much needed blunt.

I was shocked to hear that Dot told Kaymee she could sleep on a park bench. What type of mother would say some shit like that knowing how these fools were acting up in this city? That right there told me that my bestie needed to get away from her mama before she destroyed her.

I hadn't received any calls from Kaymee informing me if she was in any type of trouble, so I knew she was good. That happened two weeks ago. I talked to her via text and, briefly, on the phone. She told me that Dot put her on punishment and she couldn't come outside. I was trying to figure out how the hell she put her on punishment and she was damn near grown. Kaymee would be eighteen in exactly three weeks and I couldn't wait.

Talking to my parents about her situation, only made my mom want to go kick a hole in Dot's head. My dad had to calm her down because she was trying to go to their house. I understood how my mom felt because I was mad, too. Kaymee didn't deserve to be treated this way. I couldn't wait for her to call and say those magical words I wanted to hear.

I shook the thoughts of Kaymee to the back of my mind as I rolled over to bother my man. Waking up beside him was the best feeling for me early in the morning. He was knocked out from all of the alcohol that he consumed the night before. We went to the club and had the time of our lives. I hadn't had that much fun in a while and it was much needed.

Staring at Monty sleeping so peacefully, I let my eyes take in all of his features. He had the bushiest eyebrows and they were sexy. His light skin tone was smooth and free of any razor bumps, his goatee was lined to perfection, and his hair was cut low. His waves stood out so much that you could get seasick looking at them and his lining was on point.

I ran my hand over his chest, outlining his tattoos. He had different tribal designs across his chest, going all the way down his arms. His tattoos were so sexy to me. They were one of the things that drew me to him, not to mention the fact that he was fine.

As I continued to rub his chest, I noticed the sheet moving slightly. I glanced down to his midsection and saw his member growing by the second. A devilish grin appeared on my lips with nothing but naughty thoughts invading my mind. Easing under the sheet, I positioned my head above his thighs. I breathed in deeply and took in the faint aroma of his *Polo Black* body wash. The scent always aroused me, but only when I was around him.

My tongue had a mind of its own and it started licking his shaft from the bottom to the tip. I changed my position until my mouth hovered above his mushroom head. Placing his joint in my mouth, I sucked lightly. Monty started shifting a little bit. I began to lower my head until the tip hit the back of my throat, then I closed my lips around him and went to work.

I was sucking his dick with so much aggression that I had spit seeping out the corners of my mouth. Slurping up every drop, I ran my tongue along the base and gagged on it. I massaged his balls as I sucked harder, feeling my kitty spring to life. Rising higher on my knees, I made sure I turned my head to the left because the hook of his dick was guiding me in that very direction.

"Mmmmm, shit!" he growled softly.

I threw the covers from over my head because it was getting hot as hell under there. Gazing up into his face, I noticed that he hadn't opened his eyes. That meant that he wasn't fully awake and I wasn't doing what I set out to do. Shifting my position, I turned my body so both of my feet were on the side of his head. If I executed this correctly, things were going to turn out the way I anticipated.

I placed his tool back in my mouth and slid his dick down my throat effortlessly. Bobbing my head up and down, I sucked like my life depended on it. I felt his hand on the back of my head and he helped the movements every time I suctioned him. I observed his toes twitching and after a while, they started curling toward the ceiling.

"Yes, suck yo' dick, baby. Get that shit!"

As I heard his words of encouragement, I started putting everything into it. He moved his hand to my ass, running his fingers between my cheeks. When he started rubbing my second set of lips, my eyes closed and I paused for a moment. That slight touch felt exceptional.

"Nah, don't stop now. Yo' ass started and you will finish," he said, slapping my left ass cheek.

The sting of the impact had me leaking like a faucet. I'm glad my skin was dark because if it weren't, his handprint would be visible without a doubt. He went back to playing in my twat and I loved every minute of it. I went back to polishing off his knob and the moans and groans that left his throat were sexy. I was wetter than the Mississippi river.

"Back that ass up, baby. Put that pussy on my face," he said, patting my thigh and pulling it towards his mouth at the same time.

I didn't waste any time placing my second set of lips on top of his mouth. His tongue was nice and wet when it connected to my clit. I couldn't quite concentrate on pleasing him. All I could do was hold his member in my throat.

"Suck that shit, Poe. Stop playing with it. I already know what that mouth do and the shit yo' ass doing ain't it," he said, slapping my cheek once more.

I started sucking his dick like a baby drinking from a bottle. I was aiming to milk him for all of his babies and he was going to be on the same shit. Whenever we were in the sixty-nine position, it turned into a "who's going to tap out first" match.

Wrapping his lips around my clit, he sucked on it hard as hell. He knew that was the way I liked it to be done. Letting it go for a second, he flicked his tongue back and forth fast like he was a snake. Sticking his tongue deep into my tunnel, I felt the tingling sensation in my stomach. I pulled my pussy from his face so I could regroup. I almost came but I wasn't ready to do that.

"If you don't bring my shit back up here, we are gon' have a muthafuckin' problem," he barked, pulling my hips back toward his head.

While moving my bottom back, I took a couple quick breaths to get myself together. He snatched my hips and plopped my kitty back on his mouth. I grabbed his python and stroked it a little bit before I went back to sucking the skin off it. He stopped sucking and moved his head back and forth. It was obvious he couldn't concentrate on two things at once.

A smile formed on my lips while I continued to service my man. It didn't last long because he locked my legs in a death grip, eating my cookies like it was a gourmet meal. There was no way I could continue handling that dick. I sat up slightly and started grinding on his lips. The friction I felt between my legs had me on temporary high.

"Oh, damn! Yes, daddy!" I placed my hands on his stomach to balance myself.

My head fell back and I continued to grind. I felt his tongue stiffen. I knew what time it was then. I pulled my legs up to my chest and planted my feet on the bed. I rode his tongue the minute it was deep in my tunnel. I hadn't been in that position a full minute before my juices coated his chin. He didn't stop assaulting my clit and that took me further over the edge.

"Ahhhhhh, baby. What are you trying to do to me? Shit! I love you, Montez!"

Giving my kitty one last kiss, he let my legs go and eased from under me. I flopped on the bed and curled up. He didn't care that my legs were shaking. He turned me over and positioned himself between my legs, rubbing his tool up and down my slit. He eased into my wetness and groan heavily.

"Grrrrrrr! Damn, this pussy good as fuck! It's gripping my shit like a muthafucka!" he said, pumping in and out.

The hurting he was dishing out was one for the books. He was handling my ass, too, balling me up like I was a contortionist. It was good I was a cheerleader in high school and was flexible. If not, I would be on my way to the hospital because my joints would be popped out of place.

"Shit, Monty baby!" I screamed out. I put my hand on his stomach trying to stop him from going any deeper.

"Move yo' hand, girl. This is what that morning wood feels like. It's what you wanted, right?" he asked with a smirk on his face.

The sweat on his chest made his tattoos glisten every time the sunlight hit them. Monty released me from the hold he had on me and flipped me over. I didn't know where he got all this energy from, but I loved every minute of it.

"Toot that ass up, ma. I want your back arched just right and you bet not run for this dick!"

He ran his dick along the crack of my ass. At first, I thought he was about to try to go in that forbidden hole. I turned my head and shot him the look of death. Monty knew that was a game we weren't playing.

"What are you looking at me like that for?" he asked, laughing. "Ain't nobody trying to bust yo' ass in the booty. Chill out and get ready to cum on this muthafucka."

"Don't play with me, Montez. I will beat yo— Aaaaaaaah!" was the last thing I could say before he plunged all nine inches of that dick in my kitty.

He shut my ass up quickly. I guess I was talking too much for his liking. The grip he had on my waist was one I couldn't get out of. He was hitting spots I didn't know could be reached during sex. I felt every thrust in my soul, my legs going numb. I couldn't feel nothing except the cum that was sliding down between my thighs.

"Sssssss! Fuck Me Daddy! Shit!" I moaned loudly.

I finally got the feeling back in my legs and the only sound that could be heard was skin slapping against skin. I reached down playing with my clit, rubbing it vigorously against my fingertips. My body started shaking slightly, but I didn't stop the rhythm that I had going between my legs. Monty was pounding me hard from behind. I knew he was almost at his peak, because I was right there with him.

"Oh shit! I'm about to cum, daddy!" I cried out.

"Let that shit go then. I'm right there with you, baby!"

Both of us were breathing like we had asthma. The feeling in my stomach was building stronger. I rubbed one out last time and Monty never stopped stroking. My walls clamped down on his joint, my pussy exploding and wetting him up along with the bed.

"Yeahhhhhhh, fuck yeah!" I cried out.

"Grrrrrrr! Damn! Aaaaaaaah, yeah! Mmmmm."

Both of us came at the same time. I collapsed with him falling right on top of me. It was hard for me to catch my breath because his heavy ass was on top of me, but I didn't even have the strength to complain. I closed my eyes and drifted off to sleep. Neither one of us were worried about the wet spot that day.

***

Monty and I slept for another three hours after that sex session we had. I woke up to the smell of bacon, but I couldn't open my eyes. My body was drained. I was glad I was on birth control because his ass was trying to go half on a baby. We had been having sex for years, but there was something different about that morning.

I climbed out of bed and put on one of Monty's shirts so I could freshen up. I opened the door and walked down the hall to the bathroom. Turning the shower on to let the water temperature get just how I liked it, I grabbed my toothbrush. Brushing my teeth and washed my face while looking in the mirror, my hair was all over the place because of our rendezvous. I didn't know what I was going to do with it.

Pulling the shirt over my head, I stepped under the showerhead and let the water cascade down my body. The hot water had the bathroom steamed up and relaxed my body, as well. Once my hair was thoroughly wet, I washed it then lathered my loofah. The shea butter and coconut-scented body wash that I loved so much filled my nostrils. I washed my body twice before I stepped out of the shower.

"Oh shit!" I yelped.

Monty was standing in front of me with a huge dry towel opened for me to step into. He wrapped it around my body and kissed me deeply on the lips. I leaned into his body, deepening the kiss, getting lost every time our tongues touched. I pulled back from the kiss and looked up at him.

"You scared the hell out of me, bae. I didn't know you were in here," I said with a pout on my face. But that all changed when I thought about the kiss he had laid on me. "And what was that kiss all about?"

"I need a reason to kiss my woman now?" he asked with a raised brow.

"No, you don't. I was just asking because I think the loving I put on ya got you feeling some kind of way," I said, laughing.

"Get yo' ass outta here with that shit. The loving ain't got shit to do with nothing. It's the woman as a whole that got this nigga's nose wide open. Don't try to use that shit to your advantage, because it's not gonna work," he said, smacking me on my ass.

"Yeah, a'ight. Whatever you say."

I walked down the hall to the bedroom leaving his ass standing in that hot ass bathroom. I grabbed my Shea butter lotion off the dresser and squeezed a little in my hand. Monty walked in the room and stared at me with lust in his eyes.

"Damn, you're gorgeous," he said, licking his lips.

"Stop looking at me like that. We are not about to start nothing at this moment. I'm ready to eat some of that good food I smell coming from the kitchen. My stomach is in my back and my baby knew I would need something to eat after that workout this morning," I said, cheesing from ear to ear.

When he didn't respond to what I said, I glanced up at him. He was standing there with a stupid look on his face. Walking to the bed, he started removing the sheets. My eyes were fixated on every movement he made because I was wondering what his problem was.

"Montez, did you hear what I said?" I asked.

"Yeah, I heard what you said. Would you be upset if I told you that Dray cooked for himself and nobody else? That wasn't me in there cooking, love."

The shit he said pissed me off. How the fuck could he let a muthafucka cook in his kitchen and not cook for every damn body? I walked to my overnight bag that was sitting on the chair by the window. I took out my maxi dress and sandals along with my blow dryer, ignoring his ass. I placed my dress on the back of the chair and grabbed the dryer. There were no words I wanted to say to him at all. I was hungrier than a muthafucka, but he wanted to change the sheets.

I walked to the dresser and plugged the dryer into the outlet, sitting it down. Grabbing the comb, I sectioned my hair off and put it in three ponytails. I moistened my scalp with coconut oil with the deepest scowl on my face.

"Baby, what do you want to do—"

Before he could finish his statement, I picked the dryer up and turned it on high. Drowning his ass out, I stared at him evilly through the mirror. If he didn't know how heated I was, he would find out soon enough. Talking to him at that point was a no go. I saw him walking towards me but I didn't address him. Instead, he snatched the plug out of the wall.

"Why the hell would you do that?" I screamed irritably.

"Why the hell are you mad? Yo' ass forever getting mad over little shit. Bring yo' ass in the kitchen so you can eat! Witcho hungry ass," he said, throwing the cord to the floor.

Now I was the one standing there looking stupid. I didn't play when it was time to eat and he knew that. I don't know why he thought it was cool to play with me like that, with his ugly ass. I grabbed my dress and put it on, slipping my feet in his Nike slides. I was dressed in a flash with my three ponytails on top of my head.

I stepped into the kitchen and Monty was sitting my plate on the table. He didn't say anything to me, but he did roll his eyes though. I walked over to where he was standing at the stove and gave him a kiss on the cheek.

"Thank you, baby, and I'm sorry," I said lowly.

"Don't let that shit happen again. You know damn well ain't nobody cooking in this bitch but me," he said without turning around. "Aye, Dray! Food ready!" he hollered out loud.

Dray appeared in the doorway shirtless with basketball shorts on and he was bodied up. Kaymee better get on that and stop playing. This brother was all that and then some. I wasn't lusting over him but obviously, I stared a tad bit too long.

"Damn, brah. Get up and go put on a shirt. You see my lady sitting there, right?"

Dray looked up at him and nodded his head. "I understand, fam. No disrespect intended."

He got up and went to the guest room where he was sleeping. I sat down and started to eat, but I felt like someone was staring at me. Turning around, I was met with Monty's intense glare. I didn't know why he was looking at me in that manner but he was scaring the hell out of me.

"What Montez?"

"The next time I see you lusting over another nigga, I'm gonna hurt yo' muthafuckin' feelings," he snarled.

I was clueless as to what he was talking about. I wasn't lusting over nobody, so I didn't know where the hell that came from. "Who was I lusting over? You are exaggerating shit, Montez. I don't have eyes for anybody but you, so you can stop that shit."

"Don't sit there with that innocent look on your face, Poe. I watched you from the moment that nigga sat down. Your eyes never left his chest. I was waiting for your eyes to go lower. I was ready to slap the fuck out of you. Don't play with me!"

"You are overreacting for real. Calm yo' ass down over there and come sit down and eat. I still have my hair to do," I said, scooping eggs into my mouth.

Dray walked back in with a tank top on, but that shit didn't take from his appearance at all. His muscles were still bulging. Still, my focus was on the food in front of me. I knew better than to try that shit a second time.

"Hey, have y'all seen Kaymee?" Dray asked. "I've been texting back and forth with her but I haven't seen her. Every time I ask her to go out, she has an excuse."

"Nah, I've asked her if she wanted me to come pick her up but she always says no," Monty said.

This was the conversation that I dreaded having. I've talked to Kaymee but I didn't know what was going on with her. She hadn't been to work in three weeks and she wouldn't tell me why. I know she said that Dot had her on punishment, but that didn't have shit to do with her job. Whenever Monty would ask about her, all I could say was that she's good because that's what she told me.

"Baby, she hasn't been to work either. The manager asked if she was okay. I told her yes, too. Obviously, she has a statement that excused her from work."

"If something was wrong, I'm quite sure she would've called. Dot ain't stupid by a long shot. I told her that night what would happen to her if anything happened to Mee.

"I'm worried about her because we haven't physically seen her even though we have talked to her. Come to think about it, she was only texting the first week," Dray explained.

What he said made sense. It wasn't like Kaymee not to call, especially with me. I thought about it a little longer and got up to retrieve my phone. As I entered the bedroom, it started ringing. Tokyo Vanity's "That's My Best Friend", blared out. "Speaking of the devil," I said to myself. I rushed to the nightstand and accepted the call.

"Hey, bestie. We were just talking about you. How are you doing?" I asked, walking back to the kitchen.

"I'm doing alright. Look, I didn't call for a long drawn out conversation. I have something to tell you and I want to apologize first."

"Why would you have to apologize to me?" "Would you shut the fuck up? I don't have long to be on this phone, so would you hear me out please?" she all but yelled.

"Yeah, go ahead," I said, peering at Monty.

"Who is that?" he mouthed.

"Kaymee," I mouthed back.

"You may as well put the phone on speaker, friend. I'm not trying to explain it again to bro, I heard you trying to whisper my name. It's okay. I'm tired of hiding."

I put the phone on speaker and looked up at Monty. "It's on speaker. Go ahead," I told her.

"I'm sorry that I didn't tell y'all before now, but Dot was watching me like a hawk. Monty when you left my house a couple weeks ago, Dot beat my ass." She paused.

"She did what?" Monty asked, grabbing the phone. He was seething after hearing the words that Kaymee said.

"Hold on, Bro. Let me finish please. She was upset because I told you about her making me pay rent. I did what you told me to do and went to my room without saying anything to her. She followed me and sucker punched me while I was taking my shoes off. I was no match for her. She was fucking me up. I finally got her off me and was about to hit her in the head with a bat, but her friend Damon snatched it from me."

Monty and Dray jumped up at the same time. I already knew what was about to happen. We were going to Kaymee's house. As I was walking to the room to change and put my hair in one ponytail, I heard Monty yelling.

"Did that nigga put his hands on you, Mee?" I held my breath and prayed she said no, because if he did, his ass was good as dead.

"No, he helped me actually. He was the one that took me to the hospital. Dot went to her room and laid down."

"Pack yo' shit. I'm on my way to get you!" he screamed into the phone.

"Hurry up before she comes back. I want to be out of here before she returns," she said with a slight shake in her words before she hung up.

Monty was breathing like a kimono dragon. He was ready to lay hands on somebody. The last thing I needed to hear was him catching a body. There was no way I would be able to talk him out of fucking anybody up at that point. He was enraged and there was no coming back until he fucked somebody up.

MEESHA

Chapter 9
Kaymee

It had been two weeks since the fight between Dot and I, or should I say the unanimous decision match. My face had cleared up for the most part, but I still had bruising along the left side of my face. My right eye still had the blood clot in the corner and it was bright red. The hole in my tongue was closed somewhat, but still hurt terribly. I had to constantly rinse my mouth with salt water. My side didn't hurt too badly but I still had to keep it wrapped. The headaches were about the only thing that ceased. I couldn't sleep without waking up numerous times throughout the night. It took a while, but it doesn't bother me anymore.

I sat by the window most days, looking out to see what the fuck was going on around this dump. All I'd seen for the past few weeks was females fighting over a good for nothing nigga, crack heads running back and forth, and the rats playing tag with the cats. I was tired of being in this house listening to Dot talk shit. One thing I can say though is she hasn't brought her ass in my room with it.

Every time I go anywhere near the door, she stands in the hall hollering, "Don't go out my muthafuckin' door, bitch." I don't have time for that. The first week I didn't talk to anyone. Instead, I would send out text messages just so they would know that I was okay. Now, I was ready to go. I refused to live my life like I did something wrong when I knew I didn't.

Dot didn't want me to leave because she knew Monty was going to tap that ass. I spared her ass for two weeks. Now, it was time to put it all out on the table. That's my mama but it was time for me to stop giving a fuck about what would happen to her if I told. Shit, she didn't give two fucks about me.

I heard her talking on her phone, her voice getting closer to my bedroom. When she appeared in the doorway, I acted like I didn't know she was standing there. I really didn't care what she wanted to say. I was over everything that had to do with Dot.

"She sitting here in the muthafuckin' window looking like a muthafuckin' throw away," she said to whomever she was talking to. "I know she bet not think about it. I'll beat the fuck out of her again. Hold on, I'm about to let her ass know right now."

She put the phone down to her side and put her other hand on her hip. I still didn't turn completely around, but I saw her out of the corner of my eye. I just wanted her to say what she had to say and move the fuck around. Her ass been in this house sober as fuck for the past two weeks and haven't said ten words to me. I guess today was the day to pick on Kaymee for old times sake.

"I'm about to go out for a while. I don't want yo' ass to leave this house for nothing. I don't want nobody in my shit either. If I find out you did any of the two, yo' ass is mine. Is that understood, bitch?"

I responded to her ass with a head nod. I was almost eighteen years old and she felt like she could tell me what the fuck to do. It's cool, though. That was going to be the last time she called herself giving me a rule to follow. Once she left, I was gone.

She stood there for a minute or two longer before she left out of the doorway. I listened for the front door to open and close, then I jumped up and grabbed my phone. I had to call Poetry to tell her what the fuck I had been through. She answered on the third ring. I was so happy when she did. I was trying to start the conversation by getting everything out as quickly as possible, but her ass kept asking questions and shit. I had to tell her to shut the fuck up and let me talk.

I had her to put the phone on speaker because I knew she was around Monty. Poetry couldn't whisper for shit in the world. I heard when she tried to say my name without me knowing. I told them what went down that night and Monty was mad as hell.

"Pack yo' shit. I'm on my way to get you!" was the last thing he said to me. I don't know if he heard when I screamed for him to hurry up or not, but I threw the phone on the bed and ran to the closet. I started snatching clothes out of the closet and onto the bed. I believed that was going to be my only chance to get out of this house. I was going to make the best of it.

I had three duffle bags, an entire luggage set, and my book bag packed in a manner of thirty minutes. I was in the process of packing my makeup and toiletries when I heard constant banging on the front door. I stopped what I was doing, making a beeline to open the door. I unlocked the door and opened it. Poetry, Monty, and Dray stormed in, looking around.

"Where that bitch at, Mee?" Monty said, walking down the hall.

"She left about half an hour ago. I don't know when she will be back, so we gotta get out of here," I said, rushing to my bedroom.

Monty came in my room behind me. I went back to packing all of my makeup in a cosmetic bag and was snatched upright. He held me by my shoulders and turned me around. I grimaced with pain and doubled over a bit because he tweaked my ribcage.

"I'm sorry, sis. I didn't mean to hurt you. I need to make sure you're straight," he said, staring in my face as he turned it back and forth.

"I'm fine, bro. I swear," I said, going back to packing.

"Come here one more time, Mee. Stick out yo' tongue."

I did what he asked and his nostrils flared. His eyes turned from hazel to a dark green. I've known this man a long time and that was a true indication that he was angry.

Poetry came over and hugged him. That was her way of calming him down. It wasn't working.

"Poetry, can you pack my shoes in that bag that's on the bed, please? We have to hurry up. I don't know when she will be back," I said, panicking.

"You don't have to rush and pack shit! You gon' take every muthafuckin' thing you bought with yo' money outta this bitch! I don't give a fuck how long it takes," Monty yelled at me.

"Monty, where are we going to put everything if it's four of us and all of my things? I don't need to take all of this stuff. All I want is my belongings. The furniture can stay. It was going to stay when I left for college anyway."

"Okay, I hear you on that. Take your time packing yo' shit. You do not have to be scared of this bitch. Ain't shit happening while I'm here. I want to see her try that shit in my presence. She is already gettin' the shit slapped out of her!"

I was trying to pack my shit fast as hell but it seemed as if I was moving slower than a snail. Dray kept looking at me like he wanted to come over and hug me or something. But he stayed posted up at the entrance of my bedroom door. Poetry finished packing my shoes, coming out of the closet with three shoeboxes.

"Best friend, are you taking these?" she asked.

The boxes could stay, but I needed the contents that it held. I took the boxes from her and emptied them out on the bed. I had several stacks of money wrapped in rubber bands lying on my bed. I took one of my huge purses, threw the stacks inside, and zipped it up.

Poetry stood staring at me, not wanting to voice what was on her mind I guess. But Monty didn't hesitate, as usual speaking on what he saw. "Mee, what the fuck are you doing with all of that money in this house? You know this bitch is shiesty as hell and can smell money a mile away."

"I had to hide it in here. She watches my bank account like she makes deposits in it every two weeks. I put just enough money into my bank account so she would think she was taking all of my money. The rest went in my shoeboxes. She knew that I kept all of my shoes boxes just because and she never thought to check them. My mattress, dresser drawers, and my purses were the things she checked for money. I've been saving money for two years without her knowing," she said with a smirk.

"That a girl. I'm glad you were smart enough to do just that. I'm proud of you, sis."

When he finished what he was saying, I heard the front door open, then slammed shut. I knew Dot was back home and shit was about to get real. Dray stood at the door. I heard her yelling before she made her way down the hall.

"Who the fuck is you? I told this bitch not to have nobody in my damn house! Her ass couldn't wait for me to leave so she could sneak your ass in here to be a hoe, huh?"

Dot was talking reckless the entire time it took her to get to my room. When she got to the door, she tried to come in. Dray didn't budge. He wasn't letting her get past him. She looked up at him with her hands balled into fist. At first glance, it appeared as if she was going to hit him, but she didn't attempt it.

"Move your muthafuckin' ass out of my way, nigga! Who the fuck is you for the last fuckin' time?" she screamed at his chest.

"It doesn't matter who I am. Just know that you ain't getting in this room until she's finished doing what she gotta do," Dray said.

Monty and Poetry couldn't be seen from where Dot was standing. She could only see me still putting shit in bags. The scene before her made her even madder than seeing Dray standing in my doorway. She started trying to push her way through the door, but Dray wouldn't budge.

"Bitch, when I get in that room, I'm beating the fuck out of you! Where the fuck do you think you're going? You can pack all your shit, but you ain't going nowhere. This nigga won't be able to stop me from kickin' your ass, again," she said, laughing.

Monty stepped out into the open and she stopped struggling with Dray. I didn't say a damn thing to her. I kept getting my shit like she wasn't there. I actually slowed down because shit was about to get real in apartment 609.

"He may not be able to stop yo' ass from fuckin' her up, but I bet you a million dollars I can. I was waiting on your hoe ass to come back in this muthafucka! Didn't I tell you the last time I was here, if she called me I was gonna whoop yo' ass? I see you don't listen very well. The shit you did to her was uncalled for, Dot. She didn't deserve what you did to her, Dot," Monty said, walking towards the door.

Dot stood there looking at Monty like she was trying to find the words to throw back at him. The cat had her muthafuckin' tongue because she didn't say shit, at least not right away. She looked around a couple times, for what I didn't know. When she turned back around, her eyes were trained directly on him.

"I heard everything that you said when you brought my daughter home at damn near one in the morning. I don't give a fuck how many times she fucked and sucked yo' ass, that's still my child! There's no way you are gonna regulate what goes on in this muthafucka! I pay the bills in here!"

"You can keep right on talking out of the side of your neck. If you knew anything about your daughter, you would know that I have never touched her in that way. Mee is like a muthafuckin' sister to me. That's my woman right there," he said, pointing to Poetry who had come out of the closet when he walked to the door. "The last time I heard, you had your seventeen-year-old daughter paying the bills here. But you will have to find a way to pay that shit yo'self from now on, because she leaving this muthafucka today. If that means that I have to knock yo' ass around a little bit to get her outta here, so be it. You will not put yo' hands on her again!"

Dot started pushing Dray trying to get in, but he still wasn't letting her pass him. Monty tilted his head to the side, looking at her act a damn fool. She was kicking him, trying to bite him, and almost spit in his face. Monty allowed her to struggle with Dray a little while longer until he finally had enough of her shit.

"Let her in, fam. Don't try to keep her out no mo. Let her ass in!"

Dray moved out of the way and she came charging straight at me. Before she could reach me, Monty grabbed her by her neck and threw her against the wall. She was trying her best to get out of his grip, but it was impossible.

"Didn't I tell you not to go after her, bitch? Did I look like I was fuckin' playing with yo' hoe ass? Make me kill you in this muthafucka if you want to! You no longer have a daughter that you can manipulate and beat the fuck down!" he said, banging her head against the wall with every syllable that fell from his lips.

Poetry and I started grabbing bags as quickly as we could. Dray came over and got the luggage. There were still like five more bags, but I didn't know how we would get them out. Dray grabbed one of them and headed for the door.

"Mee, y'all get the fuck out of here. I'll get the rest of the bags," he said, never taking his eyes off Dot.

"Please don't do anything stupid, bro," I said, hesitating to leave him alone with her.

"She ain't even worth it, I promise. Go 'head and go. I got this," he said over his shoulder.

I didn't want to leave because I was afraid he was going to kill her. Poetry nudged me from behind. I finally moved my feet to leave out of the door. When I was went by Monty, Dot said something that caused me to freeze me up.

"You can leave now, but when I catch up with yo' ass again, I'm beating yo' ass. You will never make it in this world without me. You don't know shit about these streets. I don't give a fuck which one of these niggas you fuckin'. You will get eaten alive, bitch! I hope your entire life turns to shit from this day forward. When you fail, don't come crawling back to me."

After she yelled those hurtful words at me, Monty hit her hard in her face. Her head whipped to the side. He punched her again in her mouth. Blood flew out and landed on the wall. Her head hung low before he released her, letting her fall to the floor.

The words that came out of her mouth cut my self-esteem down to nothing. I looked down at her lying on the floor with tears in my eyes. I didn't want her to get hurt, but she brought that on herself. Monty scooped the remaining bags off my bed and headed to the front door. Poetry was right behind him. My mind was telling me to drop everything that was in my hands and stay, but I knew I had to get away from the toxic person that was my mother.

Chapter 10
Drayton

I couldn't believe that Kaymee's mother did her like that. When I saw her face and how she was trying to gather her clothes in pain, I wanted to rush to her side. I didn't do or say anything because I didn't want her to feel uncomfortable with me being there. We didn't know each other that well and the night we went to *Dave & Buster's* wasn't nearly enough for me to be in her business like that.

Her mama came through there acting like a wild woman. She was trying hard to get to Kaymee. I didn't know how she thought I was going to let her get past me to put her hands on my girl. A blind man could see that she had no respect for her daughter and she didn't know her at all. The things she said to her were nasty, especially coming from her own mother.

I took the bags that I grabbed down to the car. About five minutes later, everyone else walked out of the building, as well. I didn't know what happened after I left, but I was glad it was over. That shit was painful to watch without saying or doing anything.

That was two weeks ago. Kaymee went back to work and she was healing very well. All of the bruising was gone from her face and the clot in her eye was almost gone. That's the only thing that was taking its time to heal. I was glad that she was better, though.

We'd been spending a lot of time together whenever she wasn't at work. She was staying at Poetry's, but I saw her almost every day at Monty's. She always left before the curfew she and Poetry had out of respect for her parents. That was the reason I rented a car. Plus, I didn't want her riding the bus late at night either.

Kaymee showed me around the city and I loved it. It was a place I could see myself living. We went to *Buckingham Fountain* in Grant Park and took lots of pictures. That was the first time she let me kiss her. I could tell that she was nervous when the kiss ended. I didn't try to take it further than that, but I had to wait until she was ready.

Seeing the things that her mama put her through, I wasn't trying to force her into anything. I hadn't had sex since I left Atlanta and I wasn't trying to fuck a random bitch in a city I knew nothing about. So, I had to settle for beating my shit in the shower every time the urge arose.

Kaymee was at work and Poetry had the day off. We were going to check out the club where we planned to have a surprise birthday party for her next Friday. I was waiting for Monty to come back from picking Poetry up. When Poetry mentioned it was Kaymee's birthday, I wanted to do something special for her. I left it up to Poetry and Monty to get the guest list together while I took care of everything else. I even bought her a special gift that I knew she would love.

I heard a car door slam, then another. So I knew Monty was back. I walked over to the full-length mirror and made sure I looked all right. I had on a pair of black khaki shorts, a collarless black t-shirt, and my black and red Jordans. Monty and I went to the barbershop the day before and got haircuts and fresh linings.

"Yo, Dray! Where ya at, fam?" Monty yelled through the house.

"If you stop hollering and step further into the room, you would've seen me. Why the hell do you have to be so loud anyway, nigga?"

"This is my muthafuckin' house. I can do what I want to do. We don't have time for all this bitch ass complaining! We got shit to do! Bring yo' ass on. Poe, let's go!" he said, walking to the door.

I don't know why he brought his grumpy ass in the house in the first place. All he had to do was text and say come outside. He's a simple-minded ass nigga at times. I left out of the house and hit my one hitta to get my mind going. We waited outside for Poetry close to ten minutes and I could tell that Monty was irritated to the max. He opened the car door to get out at the same time she walked out of the house.

"Yo' ass know that we have to be at the club in twenty minutes, Poe! I told you to come the fuck on ten muthafuckin' minutes ago! You are gonna keep thinking what I say don't hold no merit and I'm gonna go all in on yo' ass!"

"I heard you when you said you were ready, but I had to piss! You should've come in the bathroom and wiped my pussy, nigga. You are gonna stop coming for me like you my damn daddy. That shit don't work over here!" she said, walking to the car.

"Yo' smart ass mouth gon' get you fucked up. I'm gon' show yo' ass how to stop playing with me. Don't make me force yo' ass to move around. I'll hurt yo' muthafuckin' feelings. Now get in the damn car so we can go!" He got in the car and slammed the door.

She didn't say anything else after that ass got in the front seat. Poetry fell in love with a crazy nigga that loved the hell out of her. I didn't like the way he had spoke to her but that's not my business. I won't get involved unless I see him put his hands on her, but I don't think he would cross that line. My nigga is very territorial, but I don't think he is abusive.

We made our way downtown and the traffic was thick as fuck. Monty got off the highway and took the street the rest of the way. Turning on Rush Street with three minutes to spare, he pulled into the lot. I stared at the building and the signage read "GSpot". That was a unique name for a club. We got out of the car and made our way inside.

The club was nice and classy. I loved the layout and there was more than enough space for what I had in mind. This was a twenty-one and older spot, but Monty knew the owner and he was doing us a favor. Shit, he was even throwing in a discount. I wanted to meet this nigga because you didn't have too many cats today that would do things like this for someone. Monty didn't go into detail of how he knew the dude, but it didn't matter to me.

Monty led us to the bar area and a fine chocolate chick was behind the counter. When I say that this chick was thicker than a snicker, please believe me. She had an ass that you could sit a bottle of Corona on and it wouldn't budge. She wasn't drop dead gorgeous, but she was pretty. Her almond-shaped eyes were green. That's the thing that threw me off a little. Ain't no way her black ass was born with them shits.

"Monty! Heyyy, boo. When the hell you get in town?" she shrieked, running from behind the counter. She ran straight into his arms and hugged him tightly.

I studied Poetry's facial expression and there wasn't anything glorious about it. She cocked her head to the side, all of her weight falling to the left side of her body. Her glare was dead on Monty the entire time. In her defense, she had the right to be in her feelings. He was holding on to baby girl a little too long. It seemed he forgot that Poetry was even there with him. That was not a good look.

"Ummmm, excuse me," Poetry said, still staring at them with fire in her eyes.

When Monty heard her voice, he stepped back quickly. I knew how fast she could turn from nice to a demon and this was not the time and place for it. Even though she would not be in the wrong, I really hoped she addressed the right person in this situation. He turned around towards Poetry, slightly lowering his eyes but he held his head high.

"Baby, this is Mena. Mena, this is my lady, Poetry," Monty said, introducing the two women.

Mena stared at Poetry with a smirk on her face. Something in my mind was telling me that this could get ugly. I had never seen my man shifty like he was at that moment. There wasn't a doubt in my mind that he had history with this woman. She seemed like one of those messy hoes, but I wasn't about to judge her without knowing. Soon the tension was broken when a well-dressed nigga walked up to us.

"What's up, my nigga?" he said, holding his hand out to Monty. They shook and gave each other a brotherly hug. "How long yo' ass been in town? You surprised me when you hit me up."

"What's up, G! Long time no see, big homie. I've been here over a month, but I've spending time with my girl and just chilling. We had plans to meet at the end of the month anyway, but I still should've told you I was here. I want you to meet my baby, Poetry," Monty said, reaching for her.

Poetry rolled her eyes and stepped forward. When Monty put his hand around her waist, Mena stormed off. She went back behind the counter and started fumbling with glasses loudly. G stared at her long and hard. When she looked up and made eye contact with him, she cut that shit out.

"Nice to meet you, Poetry. I hope you are keeping this chump out of trouble," he said, laughing.

"I try to keep him in line, but I can't keep my eye on him at all times. That's where the trust comes in at, right?" she said, peering in Monty's face.

Clearing his throat, "I guess so, pretty lady. That's what a strong woman does," he said, looking around a bit. "Hey, man. I'm G," he said, turning my way.

"Dray. Nice to meet you," I said, shaking his hand.

"Oh, the infamous Drayton Montgomery. I've heard a lot about you, youngin'. Don't worry. It was all good things. I want you to come to the meeting with Monty in a couple weeks. We can talk business at that time. Right now, I want to hear about this party you muthafuckas trying to throw in my establishment."

I was kind of confused as to why he wanted me at the meeting. I didn't know his ass. But I guess I would find out when the time was right. I was ready to get the party plans together before my boo got off work. I knew for a fact this was the place I wanted.

"Well my girl Kaymee is turning eighteen, I know your establishment is twenty-one and older—" I said before cut me off before.

"Dray, I didn't ask all of that. I want to know what you had in mind. The entire club will be decorated for her. There won't be any other patrons in attending. All I want you to do is to tell me how you want it to look. In case it's not sinking in, everything is on me. Kaymee is very dear to me. I won't get into that at the moment. Just know you have nothing to worry about."

He was too old to have fucked with her on any kind of relationship level, but it had me wondering what the affiliation was. I wanted to ask, but it wasn't the time to do so. I'd feel less than a man to allow G to foot the bill for my girl. I wasn't going to be able to do it.

"Thank you, G, for offering to cover all charges, but I'm a man. I have to do this on my own for my girl. She hasn't made things official yet, but I will be waiting until she does."

"I got nothing but respect for you, Dray. That's some grown man shit right there and I got to respect it. Let's sit down and talk this shit out and I'll throw some numbers out there for you," he said, leading us to a table.

I was glad Poetry was there because she knew Kaymee better than I did. I would've never been able to pull this off alone. I learned so much about her that day that I locked the information away for another day. The color theme was going to be black, silver, and green. Green was Kaymee's favorite color. We decided on black balloons with silver glitter, silver balloons with green glitter, and white balloons with black glitter. I wanted a custom banner that read

"Happy Birthday, Kaymee" in the same colors as the theme.

Poetry suggested a money case that she was going to decorate herself and a cake in the shape of the number eighteen, decorated in the exact colors of everything else. G and Monty was pleased with the suggestions as well as Poetry and myself. I was excited about the entire arrangement. I knew she was going to be surprised and very happy.

"Okay, youngin', It's time to talk numbers since you want to pay for all of this. How long are you trying to party for? I charge one hundred an hour for my spot. The club will be open from ten to four," he asked, sitting back in the chair.

I studied his face to see if he was kidding. Shit, I wanted to close the club down but six hundred for just the spot. Damn! I see I had to rethink this shit. Kaymee's gift, dress, shoes, and the diamond tiara hit my pockets hard. And I still had the decorations, cake, and not to mention, the food to consider. I think I bit off more than I could chew with this party. I didn't think it would be this expensive. My ass would be eating noodles for the next year if I went through with this shit, but I would look like a chump if I tried to back out now.

"You still with me, homie?" G asked, smiling.

He already knew that I couldn't afford this shit. "Yeah, I'm still with you. Would it be a problem if we made some adjustments? I didn't think this through. This is a little rich for my liking," I said embarrassed as fuck.

"It's all good, fam. I'll help you out with whatever you need," Monty said, speaking up before I made an ass out of myself.

"Okay, both of y'all listen to me for a minute. I owe this to Kaymee. Don't ask how because I will discuss it with her before anyone else. I know you want to do this on your own, Dray, but you're not in the position to do so. But you will be in due time. Let me cover this for you. This don't make you look like a nothing ass nigga in my eyes. I give you big ups for trying to make her day special. I got this, and I'll even allow you to take the credit. No strings attached, put your manhood in ya pocket for this one. She deserves the best for once in her life. The only thing I ask is for you to do right by her. No one but the four of us will know about this. If it gets back that you didn't make this happen, I'm beating somebody's ass."

I was skeptical about this shit. I didn't know this nigga but he seemed like an upfront muthafucka. I sat back in the seat quietly, and then I looked up at him and said two words, "Thank you."

***

This last week has been nerve wrecking. I barely had the strength to wash my ass at that moment. It had been hard hiding all of the things I had to do which caused me to spend less time with her. Kaymee was suspicious about why I was always cancelling plans. I knew this because sometimes when I texted her, she would look at that shit and keep it moving. She wouldn't respond at all. I was even sent to voicemail, but tonight was the night to put her mind at ease.

I sent her outfit with Poetry last night and we had a plan in place. I was going to go pick her up at seven, then we were going to take a horse and carriage ride. She is under the impression that we are going to a ballroom dance that I saw online. So, that would explain why she had such a fancy dress. The tiara was because she was the birthday princess for the night.

Poetry went with her to get her locs done along with a manicure and pedicure. I also paid a makeup artist to apply her makeup. I did all of that on my own. G didn't have shit to do with any of that. I couldn't wait to see her and that made me nervous, too.

I was on my way to pick up my all black Gucci suit and shoes to match. It was going to be an all-black everything night. The only color that I would have is the handkerchief that was green and silver. I will admit this one, though. G funded this shit, too. There was no way I would've been able to match Kaymee's fly any other way. I was grateful.

When I got to the tailor shop, they had everything waiting for me at the front. I had my final fitting two days ago, so I liked the fact that I didn't have to wait a long period of time. My next stop was GSpot because G wanted me to see the finished product of the club. He explained that he took care of the guest list for the most part, Poetry and Monty was inviting the rest of the people. The only thing I had to do was get her there.

It took me a good thirty minutes to get to the club because the bitch ass GPS took me along the scenic route, dumb bitch. I pulled into a space and got out. I had texted G on the ride over, letting him know that I was enroute. He was standing outside waiting for me, smoking a blunt.

"What up, Dray. Did you make it to the tailor?"

"Yeah, I made it. Thanks again, man, for looking out for a nigga. I owe you big time," I said, giving him dap.

"You don't owe me shit. I did that shit for Kaymee. I don't say that in a disrespectful way either, so don't take it like that. I feel that she deserves for this day to be special and as I said before, I won't discuss it until I talk to her first," he said, hitting the blunt, holding it out for me.

I declined his offer and stood there thinking while he finished. His status in Kaymee's life was crowding my brain. I had to ask him one question.

"Hey, G. can I ask you something?" He nodded his head yes.

"Did you have a relationship with Kaymee?" I didn't beat around the bush. I just let the question ride.

He laughed for a couple seconds and took another pull off his blunt. "Do I look like a muthafucka that needs an eighteen-year-old on my arm? Shit, she just turned eighteen today, nigga! That was an insult, but I'll let it slide because I know you won't understand until the shit unfolds and you hear the details. Until then, leave the shit alone because I'm not saying shit. To answer your question, though, no, I didn't have an intimate relationship with her. I have a wife and a kid that I love very much, that's something you don't have to worry about. Let's get in here so you can take yo' jealous ass to yo' girl," he said, chuckling and shaking his head.

We walked in and it was dark. G hit a switch and the lights came on in slews of green and silver. The shit looked like something out of the movies, it was beautiful. The tables had green, black, and silver tablecloths. There were balloons floating in the air. There were hundreds of them. The money case that Poetry purchased was decorated beautifully and it had a lock on it. I already had it in my mind that I was going to bless that muthafucka nicely.

I looked straight ahead and my breath got caught in my throat. The entire wall read, "Happy 18th Birthday, Kaymee" in italic letters with her prom picture blended into the wall. I couldn't stop looking at the image of her because she was so beautiful. She stood gracefully in a green dress that was off the shoulders. It hugged her curves perfectly, the bottom flaring out at her feet.

"What do you think?" G asked.

Breaking my eyes away from the wall, I was speechless. He brought my vision to life and I knew that Kaymee would have a smile on her face for a while after this. "I love it, man. This goes beyond my expectations. You did everything I wanted and brilliantly at that. I know you are gonna cuss my ass out, but I owe you, man," I said, throwing my arms around him.

"Get yo' ass off me. I'm a Goon, nigga!" he said, laughing. "You're welcome, youngin'."

"Thanks again, G."

"Alright, I'll see you tonight. Go home and get some sleep. We about to party like it's nineteen ninety-nine in this bitch," he said, walking me to the door.

Before I left out the door, I turned to admire the wall one last time leaving with the biggest smile on my face.

Chapter 11
Kaymee

It was my eighteenth birthday and I was excited to see how the day was going to play out. The week before was emotional for me because every time I tried to spend time with Dray, he had something to do. I knew I said that I wasn't ready for a boyfriend, but he grew on me. I figured I'd do what Monty and Poetry insisted, and that was to live a little. That's what I had been doing since I moved out of Dot's place.

I was used to being around him when I wasn't at work and for him to, all of a sudden have so much to do, rubbed me the wrong way. I didn't tell him that I wanted a relationship yet, but in my damn mind, that was my man. The thought of him being with a woman crossed my mind a couple times, but all of that came to an end that night.

I was sitting in the family room watching *Love & Hip Hop Atlanta* with Mama Chris. These women were messy as hell. Ain't no way I would be on TV embarrassing myself. Poetry came home with a garment bag and another bag, smiling like she won the lottery. She had my curiosity radar on ten. I didn't even speak to her. I just kept eyeing the items in her hands. Her mom was smiling as well and that was enough to make me speak up.

"Friend, what are you up to? You look like you are up to no good," I said, standing up from the   sofa.

"Hello to you, too, best friend. You are so rude," she said, laughing.

I didn't find anything funny. She knew better than anyone that I hate surprises. She had better start talking and she had about ten seconds to spill it. She stood there continuing to laugh, but I wasn't playing with her. She realized that shit when I didn't join in.

"Ok, dang. These things are for you. Dray sent them," she said, unzipping the garment bag.

When she pulled the dress out of the bag, my mouth hit the floor. It was beautiful. From what I could see, it was all black and short as hell. The top looked like it was made to sit off my shoulders. I had never worn anything like that before. The most elegant dress that had ever graced my body was my prom dress.

"Go try it on and make sure it fits," Mama Chris said, smiling from ear to ear. "I knew it was a reason I liked that boy. He did his thang with this dress. I want to take it for myself," she said, laughing.

"Yeah, try it on. I want to see what it looks like on your body, Big Booty Judy." I rolled my eyes at her ass. She knew I hated when she called me that. You would've thought I would be used to it by now, seeing that she's been calling me that shit from day one.

"Come on, girl! We got shit to do today. By the way, Happy Birthday, Bitch!" she screamed, running towards me. I guess she forgot her mama was sitting right there. She damn near tackled me to the floor, kissing me over my whole damn face.

"Thank you! Now get off me! Keep ya damn mouth off me, too. I know where it's been," I said, whispering the last part in her ear. But that shit was funny as fuck. That's what she got for keeping secrets and shit.

"Poetry, you better watch your damn mouth in my house. You ain't too old to get your ass knocked off," Mama Chris said, chastising her ass. "Happy birthday, Kaymee!" she said, walking over to give me a hug.

Mama Chris walked to the kitchen and came back with a small, wrapped box and a card. My eyes teared up instantly. It had been eleven years since I received a gift from an adult. Poetry and Monty always looked out for me on my birthday. Dot never celebrated my birthday. Shit, any damn holiday that required her to spend money on me. One would have thought she was a Jehovah Witness or something. But I didn't expect anything after a while and it became a part of my life like everything else.

"Open it," Mama Chris said.

I did as I was told, carefully peeling the paper off. "Girl, if you don't rip that paper off! What are you trying to save it for?" Poetry shouted.

It made me start laughing, breaking my concentration. When you are not used to getting gifts, saving everything associated with it was a must. But I went ahead and ripped the paper off. Inside was a box with the name *Pandora* on the outside. I opened the lid slowly and there was a silver bracelet lying there with a heart shaped clasp. There was a charm with a "K" on it and two others with the number one and eight on them. I lifted it up and the floodgates opened.

"Thank you so much, Mama Chris. It's beautiful," I said, hugging her.

I cried one of those ugly cries. I had never gotten a gift that expensive a day in my life. I would cherish this bracelet forever.

"You're welcome, baby," she said, rubbing my back.

I turned my head to show Poetry the bracelet and she stood there with another box held out. I didn't know how I was going to handle all of the love that was being shown to me at that moment. The tears started up once again and I couldn't do anything but let them flow. Once I checked my emotions, I reached out for the box she had for me.

She didn't bother wrapping hers, so I didn't have any paper to rip off. The gift came from *Kay Jewelers* and I was eager to see what was inside. I lifted the top and saw a silver roped chain inside. The chain had a charm in the shape of a puzzle piece that said "Best Friend". I looked up and Poetry had the same chain and charm around her neck. I didn't even notice it until then.

"Oh, thank you, best friend! I love you so much!" I said, crying in her arms.

She let me get my snot all over her shirt before letting me go. "Okay, enough of this mushy stuff. It's time for us to go. You don't have time to try on the dress, but I know it fits. I helped pick it out. I just wanted to see what it would look like. We have hair appointments, manicures, and pedicures to attend to. Dray will be here at seven o'clock sharp, so we don't have any time to waste. I'm not missing out on getting my hair done," she said, grabbing her purse and keys.

"I'm confused," I said, looking at her scramble around. "Why are you getting your hair done?" I asked her with my hands on my hip.

She paused for a second, then turned to face me. "Dray is paying, that's why. What you thought?"

I couldn't do anything but laugh. I put my shoes on and grabbed my phone before I walked to the door. Mama Chris placed my dress back in the bag while Poetry glanced down at the front of her shirt. She looked at me and shook her head.

"Give me a minute. Somebody put snot on my shirt," she said sarcastically.

I hunched my shoulders and walked to the bathroom to wash my face. When I was done, Poetry was ready to go. I skipped all the way to the car. I was on cloud nine and there wasn't anything that anyone could do to bring me down.

**

We were out getting pampered for about five hours. Dray out did himself for my day. I couldn't wait to see him. I was going to give him the biggest kiss ever. My mind was telling me to fuck him, but I was far from ready for that. He's not even my boyfriend anyway. I got my locs done and after seeing that dress, I knew I needed my hair pinned up. I let my stylist do what she wanted to do. The only thing I suggested was to dye my hair black.

She decided to give me a bun going down the middle of my head with a couple of locs cascading down my temples. I loved it. Poetry got a Brazilian blowout, causing her hair to flow sexily down her back. Couldn't anyone tell us that we weren't the shit. Our next destination was to get our nails and feet done.

With the way that woman was massaging my feet, I damn near fell asleep on her ass. It felt so good and I needed that treatment. Running around Walmart for hours did a girl's feet so wrong, but Ling was getting all the kinks out of them bad boys. When she finished, I was kind of upset because I didn't want it to end.

"You want color?" she asked.

"No, I want a simple French manicure, please."

Poetry walked over with three bottles of nail polish in her hand. She was walking on the heels of her feet so she wouldn't mess up her toes. I looked at her wondering what in the hell she was doing. "Ling, give a French manicure on all of her toes, but I need a pretty design on the big toes with these colors," she said, handing Ling the bottles.

"Is that what you want?"

Poetry looked at her with a disgusted look on her face. "Do what I told you to do, please! She doesn't have a say so today. Listen sometimes," she said, rolling her eyes going back to her seat.

My best friend was crazy as hell. Ling did what she was asked and after she was finished, we got our fingernails done. The same thing happened as Poetry wanted those same color designs on my ring fingers. I didn't question her. She obviously knew more about my birthday plans than I did. The colors actually went very well together and I liked the way it turned out. Once we got our eyebrows arched, we were done.

Back in the car, I looked at the time. It was four o'clock. That would give me time to take a nap. I was tired as hell. My body felt relaxed and I was looking good, my brows were on point. The only thing that was missing was my makeup. I'd deal with that when I woke up to get dressed. I decided to take a shower before I laid down to nap, so I wouldn't be rushing to get ready once I got up.

I'm gonna take a nap when we get back to the house. I'm beat," I said, glancing at Poetry while she drove.

"That's fine. You have a glam session at six anyway, so you have plenty of time," she said nonchalantly as fuck.

"What are you talking about now, Poetry?"

"Someone is coming to the house to do your makeup at six. What didn't you understand?" she asked smartly.

I couldn't believe Dray arranged all of this just for me! I saw a different side of him and I liked what I'd seen so far. He was definitely boyfriend material. I just hope he wasn't doing all of this because he thought he was getting some pussy. *Shidddd, he might,* I thought in my head. I would hate to have to hurt his feelings if that was what he thought.

We pulled into the driveway and I jumped out as soon as the car stopped. I took my key out of my purse and went inside. I went straight to my room and started stripping. I wrapped my head in a scarf and put on a shower cap so my locs wouldn't get wet. Walking into the bathroom, I turned the shower on so the water temperature could heat up. When it was nice and hot, I got in thoroughly washing and rinsing my body. I was ready to sleep, so I had to wash my ass thoroughly because there wasn't about to be a second wash. I got out and took the shower cap off, hanging it on the caddy. Drying off, I walked into the bedroom and jumped in the bed. Getting deep under the covers, I buried my head and was out like a light.

"Kaymee. Wake up, sweetie. Your makeup artist is here. Kaymee!"

I heard Mama Chris's voice, but my eyes wouldn't open to save my life. My body was tired from lack of sleep. Staying up half the night trying to figure out what Dray was up to all week had caught up to me. I rolled over, stretched my body, and turned back around fluffing my pillow.

"Kaymee, get yo' ass up now!" she yelled.

Sitting straight up in the bed with the covers pulled to my chin, I sat very still. When she yelled like that, I won't lie, I thought I was back at Dot's house. After what she did to me a couple weeks back, I was scared of every damn thing. I looked at her until my eyes focused and I could see her face clearly, my heart no longer hammered in my chest.

"I'm up." I said taking a deep breath. "Where will she be working?"

"He is in the dining room. I'll tell him to give you a few minutes," she said, walking out.

I went to the bathroom to wash my face and brush my teeth. I also cleansed my face beforehand. Walking back into the bedroom, I put on my robe and a pair of socks. Stretching one more time, I made my way to the dining room to get my face beat to the gods.

When I got to the dining room, there was a man sitting waiting on me. I smiled because I knew that my makeup was about to be on fleek! I'd seen plenty men on *YouTube* doing makeup and most of them do that shit better than women. There wasn't any doubt in my mind that he wouldn't do a miraculous job.

"Hello, I'm Jason. It's a pleasure to meet you, Kaymee," he said, holding out his hand.

I didn't mean to, but I stared down at his hand once it touched mine because it was softer than a baby's ass. Let's talk about his nails. They looked better than mine. "Those are cute! Who does your nails?" Before I knew it, the words were out of my mouth. I hope he didn't get offended.

"I go to the shop on seventy-ninth and Constance. Ask for Sasha. I've been going to her for years. Tell her that I recommended you. She will hook you up," he said, waving his hand around with every word.

"Thank you. I sure will," I said, sitting down.

"Would you mind going to get dressed so I would know exactly what I'm doing to that beautiful face, girl?" he said, crossing his legs.

"Not at all. I'll be right back," I said, getting up to go back to my room.

I took the garment from the back of the door. I saw it when I came in earlier, so I didn't need to bother Mama Chris or try to figure out where it was. Unzipping the bag, I removed the dress and laid it out on the bed. My boobs were big but they didn't sag, so I figured I could pull this baby off without a bra. I took off my robe and oiled my body up before I slipped the dress over my head.

I walked out of my room and to Poetry's. When I knocked, she didn't answer. Walking a little further down the hall, I knocked on Mama Chris's door. Stan, Poetry's dad, came to the door. He smiled at me and I blushed. I'd always thought her daddy was fine, but I looked at him as a father figure, first and foremost. But I didn't know he was even home. Otherwise, I wouldn't be standing in front of him holding my dress up in the front. I was very uncomfortable.

"Well hello, beautiful. Happy birthday!" he sang out.

"Thank you, Stan. Um, is Mama Chris awake? I need help with my dress," I said shyly.

She must've heard me because she appeared in the doorway. "What's going on, Kaymee?" she asked.

"I can't zip my dress and Poetry is sleeping. I didn't know Stan was home. I'm sorry."

"You didn't do anything wrong. There's nothing to be sorry about," she said, walking behind me.

Stan had walked back into their bedroom while Mama Chris zipped my dress up. She adjusted my boobs in the dress so they would sit properly. It felt awkward because I'd never had anyone touch any part of my body other than myself.

"I'm sorry for touching you, but you have to be perfect tonight and I'm going to make sure you are. You are beautiful, baby," she said once she was finished.

I couldn't do anything but smile. She walked back to the dining room with me and when we walked in, Jason looked up from his phone. His eyes lit up and he started clapping loudly.

"Yassssss, ma! You are wearing the hell out that dress! You better werk, baby! You. Better. Werk!" he screeched, snapping his fingers. "Turn around so I can see."

I did as he asked. I thought he was going to fall into a death drop right there in the middle of the floor. "Girl! You did that!" he cheered, clapping again like a proud mama.

Poetry came out of her room to see what all of the commotion was about. She took one look at me and both her and Jason were carrying on loud as hell. The main topic between them was the way the dress hugged my ass. I couldn't stand them, but I found myself blushing and laughing right along with them fools.

"Okay, it's time for me to do my magic. I was told to give you a nude look with smoky eyes, and green and silver eye shadow," Jason asked.

I wasn't about to lie, I didn't know what the fuss was all about with those colors. Everybody knew but me, so I just shrugged my shoulders. That only made him turn to Poetry and she shook her head "yes". I rolled my eyes and closed them. Once Jason started, he didn't stop until he was done and it didn't even take him long. He handed me a mirror and I was in awe. He blended the colors perfectly, the foundation being my color to the T. The nude lip color was something that I had never thought about, but it will be added to my collection from this day forward. The lashes that he applied to my eyes weren't too long or too short. They were just right. I couldn't stop blinking.

"Oh my Gosh! Thank you so much! I love it!" I said, glancing up at him.

"My pleasure, hunty. I heard it's your birthday," he said with his hand on his hip, batting his eyelashes.

"Yes, it is!"

"Well since you are so beautiful—Nah, bish. You are fabulous! I have an entire birthday makeup case for you, chile. I want you to cherish this, girl! It has everything a diva will need to keep the face on, you hear me. And if you ever need any help at all, don't hesitate to call me my card is in the case. If I can't get to you, I am only a Facetime call away. But I want you to enjoy your birthday, and I will see you again soon, boo," he said, giving me a couple air kisses.

"Thank you so much, I appreciate it," I said, starting to tear up.

"If you cry, our friendship will be over before it even begins. Don't you dare!"

I stopped those tears and grabbed a napkin off the table before I could even spear the makeup. When I dabbed at my eyes, I looked down at the napkin and nothing was on it. I was confused as to why it didn't come off. I kept staring at the napkin like the makeup would magically appear.

"I knew that you would be doing that tonight, so all of your makeup is waterproof. The only thing you may need to touch up is your lips. Thank me later. I have to go. I have a date," he said, closing his supplies.

Mama Chris showed him to the door for me. I had fifteen minutes to finished getting ready. I rushed in my room and grabbed the other bag that Poetry brought in. There were two boxes in it. One I knew were shoes and the other was a round box. I placed the round box on the bed and I opened the shoebox. I pulled out a pair of silver open-toed stilettos and I fell in love with them on sight. The heels were green. I had never seen anything like them.

The thought of those colors came to mind once again. But that was a thought for another day, I had to get a move on before Dray showed up. I placed the shoes on my feet, feeling like Cinderella at the ball. I stood and twirled around twice, giving myself a hug.

Poetry and Mama Chris walked in holding their presents. I held my wrist out so Mama Chris could put the bracelet on while Poetry put the charmed, best friend chain around my neck. I turned to the full-length mirror and the person that looked back at me was one I didn't recognize at all. She was beautiful. It was at that moment, I realized I still had on my headscarf. I took it off and my hairstyle brought everything to life. I couldn't stop smiling.

"Open the last box, friend," Poetry said.

I had forgot all about the box I sat to the side. Walking to the bed, I lifted the lid and once again, I was met with another beautiful gift that had my mouth hanging open. There was a diamond tiara with a single emerald gem in the front sitting on a black satin pillow, the trimmings around the pillow being green and silver. This time, I couldn't stop the tears. This was the best birthday that I'd ever had. Dray was officially my man after this shit.

"Are those real diamonds?" I exclaimed.

"I was told they were and a real emerald, too!" Poetry said, smiling.

"This is too much! I can't accept this! What did I do to deserve this?" I asked no one in particular.

"You were just being you. Don't ever change that, Kaymee," Mama Chris said, kissing my forehead.

At that moment, the doorbell rang. I got nervous and didn't even know why. I started twisting my fingers together while Mama Chris left to answer the door.

"Kaymee, everything is going to be fine. Go have a good time and you don't have to do anything you don't want to do. Dray is not on that anyway. Have fun," Poetry said, placing the tiara on my head.

The tiara sat on top of my head just like it was supposed to. I beamed with happiness all over again. It was about to be a birthday to remember. We walked to the door and Mama Chris had already answered it. There was a gentleman in a suit standing in the doorway waiting on me. I was about to leave out when Poetry ran up to me with my purse and my phone. I was so excited about leaving that I didn't think to grab those items, but I'm glad she looked out for me.

"Thanks, boo. Don't be asleep when I come in. I want to tell you all about my night," I said, hugging her.

"Oh, best believe I'm gonna be up waiting on ya," she said with a smirk on her face.

"Okay, Miss Kaymee. Your ride is waiting," the gentleman said, tipping his hat and taking a bow.

That gesture alone made me giggle. I've never seen this type of service rendered except in movies. As he held out his elbow, I took hold of it. When we starting walking I stumbled a bit. Not because I tripped in my stilettos, but from the sight of the   silver-stretched limo that was sitting in the driveway. This man of mine went all out for my birthday and I couldn't wait to see him.

The chauffeur opened the back door for me and Dray stepped out looking good! He had on an all-black tux, a black shirt that was unbuttoned, showing off his chest. My Prince was standing in front of me with a dozen roses in hand. The smile on his face showed off his pretty, white teeth. I never knew chocolate could look so good.

"Happy birthday, baby. You look beautiful," he said, bending down kissing me on the cheek.

"That's how you do that! From now on, that's how you treat my best friend!"

I turned around laughing because Poetry ignorant ass was standing on the porch jumping up and down like a fool. Mama Chris and Stan were hugged up beaming with pride. Stan gave Dray the thumbs up sign, giving his approval.

"Thank You, Mr. Glover and hello, Mrs. Glover. I'll have her back before one. Is that okay?" Dray asked Stan.

"She's a grown woman, Drayton. What times she comes back is solely up to her. What I will say is this, treat her like a lady at all times and enjoy yourselves."

"I can do that. Goodnight, everyone. We have things to do," Dray said as we waved goodbye.

Handing me the roses, he held my elbow and helped me into the limo before getting in himself. The chauffeur closed the door, then hopped in the driver's seat. Once the limo was in motion, I turned to Dray. He was gazing at me with lustful eyes. My face started heating up because I was blushing hard.

"Aren't you looking handsome tonight? You clean up well, Mr. Montgomery," I said, tweaking his chin.

"Thank you, but I don't got shit on you, ma. You are so beautiful, Kaymee. I'm gonna make this the best birthday ever for you."

"You already have! Thank you for everything, I wasn't expecting all of this. Actually, I wasn't expecting anything at all."

"The night is still young, beautiful. Get ready to have the time of your life," he said, grabbing my hand and kissing the back of it.

Chapter 12
Kaymee

Sitting in the limo, holding hands with Dray was something I'd never done. Poetry and I went to prom together, so there wasn't a guy around, but we had fun. This was different all the way around. I didn't know what I was supposed to do. I felt out of place and I was worried about this being the last time he would do something like this for me. I was thinking about the lack of experience I had in this department and about him turning his back to get a girl that knew more about men.

"Relax, Kaymee," he said, rubbing his thumb across my hand. "It's your day and I want you to enjoy yourself. Stop putting so much thought into it."

All I could do was nod my head letting him know I heard what he said, but my mind wasn't listening. It was funny that he would say that though, as if he read my thoughts. I glanced out the window and we were on Michigan Avenue. The limo came to a stop in front of the *Contemporary Museum of Photography*. I only knew that because I read the sign. The chauffeur got out to open our door and came around to help us out.

"Your first stop, Madame," he said, while taking hold of my hand.

I felt as if I was part of the Royal Family with the way I was being catered to. I was going to play the part to the end, too. I stepped onto the sidewalk waiting for Dray to get out. He stood talking to the chauffer for a few seconds as I waited patiently. A woman walked by admiring my dress.

"That dress is stunning and you are so beautiful," she said.

"Thank you," I replied with a smile.

Dray walked up to me as I finished talking to the woman with a smile on his face. I looked in front of the limo and there was a horse and carriage sitting there. Lo and behold, those damn colors were on display again. I knew it wasn't a coincidence my was my ride waiting on me.

"Are we going on a horse and carriage ride, Drayton?"

"Oh, I'm Drayton now, huh?" he asked, chuckling.

"The way you are showing out today, there will be no street names tonight. You are on your grown man shit," I shot back, blushing.

"To answer your question, yes, we are. I wanted to do something special for you and there's nothing more special than being with a beautiful woman on her birthday. Plus, I wanted everyone to see how radiant you looked all dressed up. It would be selfish of me to keep all this beauty to myself."

The words he spoke were right on time and I heard the sincerity of every syllable. Let me find out this man was laying it on thick because he likes me that much. Shit, I knew he had some type of feelings for me because if he didn't, I'd be enjoying dinner and a movie instead of all of this or maybe he would've been trying to Netflix and chill.

"Let's go. Your chariot awaits, my dear," he said, leading the way.

The driver tipped his hat and held out his hand, helping me onto the carriage. The horse smelled funny, but I didn't complain about it. I wanted to enjoy the experience. I had never ridden on a horse and carriage before. Dray climbed up and sat next to me, draping his arm over my shoulders. There was a huge gap between us, so it was kind of awkward. I broke the ice, moving closer to him and laying my head on his shoulder. He started rubbing his hand along my shoulder. I felt a tingling sensation run down my arm.

When the carriage started moving, nothing was said between the two of us. I sat up and took in the scenery. I had never been downtown at night and it was beautiful. There were lights up and down the streets that made the ride more romantic. I was in awe of all of the couples hugging and enjoying a night out on the town.

It was a great night to be out because it had cooled down a lot from earlier that the day. Five minutes into the ride, we were still trotting along the Avenue when I felt the carriage turning. Once we were headed eastbound, I knew where we were going. Dray and I had gone to *Buckingham Fountain* a couple of times and I loved it, but I'd never seen it at night. He was about to experience another first with me, and I couldn't be happier.

"I can't thank you enough for all of this, Dray," I said, looking at him.

"Well, stop thanking me then. There's none needed. It feels good to know I have a girl on my arm that appreciates what I do for her. You are one of the few that doesn't expect a man to do anything for her. In my eyes, that's a real woman and I don't mind doing whatever it takes to see you smile."

"I'm glad you see that in me because that's the way that I am. You have learned a little about my life, so you know how hard it is for me to expect something. Today was the first time since my granny passed that anyone has done something for my birthday and that was twelve years ago."

"Kaymee, I want you to put all of that behind you. The only way your past can hurt you is if you allow it to. You are about to go to college in two weeks and I will be your support every step of the way. You were the one that got yourself to where you are, nobody else. I'm willing to wait for you because you're worth it. I will not pressure you at all, babe. *We* are working on your time. What do you say about that?"

By the time I could respond, the chariot had stopped. I saw Dray looking at his phone. He was texting away. I wanted to ask who was he was talking to but that wasn't my business. He wasn't my man. I sat patiently waiting to see what the next move was going to be.

"Sorry about that. Let's go view this fountain and take some pictures. We have to head out to our final destination soon. The best is yet to come," he said with a sly grin on his face.

"Where is our final destination, if you don't mind me asking?"

It's for me to know and for you to wait and see," he said, pulling me in for a hug. His lips brushed across my cheek. I turned my head so they would connect with my lips. He pulled back at first, running his tongue over his bottom lip.

"I can get used to that. Let's go to the fountain before I have you laying across this seat," he said, getting down from the chariot.

Once I was down, he grabbed my hand and we walked to the fountain. There were many couples out that night. The closer we got to the fountain, the prettier it became. With every few seconds that passed, the fountain turned into a different color. It was a sight to see and I wanted to capture it on my phone. As I was pulling it out, a guy walked up to us with a camera around his neck. I was confused as to why because there were plenty of couples out, so why us?

"Drayton and Kaymee?" he asked with uncertainty.

"Yes, I'm Dray. You must be Stephon. I was wondering where you were. Are you ready to start shooting?"

"Yeah, my equipment is set up over there," he said, pointing to the other side of the fountain.

I didn't know what was going on. Dray never said anything about a photo shoot. Then again, I didn't know beforehand about any of the things that had happened so far today. Relaxing my shoulders, I went with it, allowing the surprises to unfold.

The photo shoot was amazing and I had fun doing it. There were a lot of great shots once I looked at all of the photos once we were done. Dray and Stephon talked about when to expect the photos back and I couldn't wait. We stood with Stephon until he had gathered all of his equipment before we went back to the chariot.

We walked towards the chariot but Dray grabbed my arm, leading me in another direction. I was puzzled until I saw our limo up the street. I got excited all over again because I was anxious to know where we were heading next.

"Thank you for the photo shoot. I felt so beautiful taking those pictures. I can't wait to see them in print. You went all out for little ol' me, Dray," I said, stopping before we made it to the limo. "I want to thank you again for all of this. I think I want to make it official between us. You proved to me that you have feelings for me. I've had feelings for you before any of this, but I was fighting them because it seemed too good to be true. But you showed me that you could make me happy better than you could ever tell me," I said, hugging him.

He bent his head down and placed his lips on mine. I deepened the kiss by giving him my tongue to taste. It was the first time I had ever French- kissed and there are many more firsts that I want to experience with him.

***

We got settled in the limo and we were off to who knew where, but I was ready for it. Dray was typing away on his phone and I was curious as hell. I didn't hide the fact that I was being nosy, so I jokingly said something.

"Who are you over there texting? Your girlfriend?"

He looked over at me with his eyebrow raised. "My woman sitting right next to me. Why would I do something like that? Don't worry your pretty little mind. I have all that I want right here," he said, patting my knee, but that didn't stop him from texting.

He put his phone inside his suit jacket pocket and turned to me. "We are almost at our location so I need you to trust me right now. Can you do that?" he asked.

"I do trust you. Why would you say that?"

He reached in his pocket and pulled out a green silk scarf. I didn't know what he wanted to do with it. The first thought that came to mind was he wanted to tie me up. I know it's funny but that's what I thought. But that went out the window because we were in the back of a limo for Christ's sakes. Plus, I was a virgin. I was far from being a freak.

"What are you gonna do with that?" I asked. I was tired of speculating about it.

"Where we are going, I want you to be amazed when you see it. It's my last surprises and I don't want you to see it coming," he explained.

As much as I hated surprises, I wanted to go along with it because he put so much thought into my day. I may as well let him go out with a bang. "Okay, I'll trust you. But you better not let me run into anything, Dray!"

"I promise you I won't. Now, turn around so I can place the scarf around your eyes."

Once the scarf was in place, I couldn't see anything. A couple minutes later, the limo came to a halt. I heard the door open and I felt Dray's hand wrap around mine. I scooted across the seat slowly, allowing him to guide me.

"Step down," he said as I was getting out of the limo.

He didn't let my hand go from that point. I was taking tiny steps because I had never given anyone that much control over my life and I was kind of scared. For one, I didn't know what was going on,] and two, I didn't hear anything around me. For all I knew, he could be taking me somewhere to take my cookies.

"We are at the curb. I need you to step up so you don't fall on your face."

I did as I was told and we continued to walk without incidence. I heard another door open. I was trying to listen for any type of sound, but I heard nothing. Wherever we were, it was cool and I felt goose bumps appearing on my arms. The air conditioning was on full blast.

"Okay, I'm about to take off the scarf. You ready?" he asked.

I shook my head yes as I felt him taking the knot out. He paused for a minute and I felt like I was about to have an anxiety attack from the suspense. He took the scarf off and all I heard was, "Happy birthday, Kaymee!" being screamed from every inch of the building. I looked around in amazement as I saw several people from school, my co-workers, Mama Chris, Stan, Poetry, Monty and many others that I didn't know at all.

"Oh, my God! How the hell did you pull this off?" I asked, turning to Dray. I then hit him in the chest before I grabbed and hugged him.

"It took a lot of work, but I did it. Happy birthday, baby. It's time to party!" he said, kissing me on my lips.

The deejay started playing 50 Cents' "In Da Club". Everyone crowded around me and started dancing. I didn't have a choice but to join in. Poetry made her way through the crowd, singing and dancing in my face.

"Go, shawty. It's your birthday. We gonna party like it's your birthday. We gonna sip Bacardi like it's your birthday. And you know we don't give a fuck, it's not your birthday," she sang, while twerking on me.

I couldn't do anything but laugh as I started twerking with her. One thing that we both loved to do was dance. When the song was over, she took my hand and I looked around for Dray but I didn't see him. My eyes took in everything about the club and those damn colors were everywhere. It made sense at that point, all the clues leading up to my party.

When I laid eyes on the wall that was in front of me, tears flowed down my cheeks because it was so beautiful. I pulled Poetry back so I could talk in to her ear. "You helped with this shit, didn't you?" She looked at me, shaking her head yeah.

I hit her on the arm and hugged her tightly. Someone came and hugged me from behind. I didn't know who it was. When I tried to turn around, they wouldn't allow me to. Then finally, I was released. I turned and there was Monty standing there looking cleaner than the board of health. He shocked the hell out of me looking like a Don around that bitch.

"Happy birthday, sis," he said, pinning a one hundred-dollar bill to my dress. "Before the night is over, that is gonna be a money dress you're wearing, and I set the standards high. These muthafuckas better come correct or not at all."

"Thank you, Monty. Let me guess, you had something to do with this too, didn't you?" I said with my hand on my hip.

"Of course, I did. That nigga Dray don't' know shit about you. Me and Poe had to help him out, but only the best for my Mee," he said, kissing my cheek. "Let's get this party started!" he yelled.

For the next couple of hours, I had the time of my life. I danced so much my feet were aching. I had taken my shoes off, replacing them with a pair of silver ballerina slippers within the first hour. After the exchange, I had been dancing since. Monty had taken all of the money off my dress because it was so much. People were pinning money on me every time I looked around. I was so grateful and surprised because I didn't know most of these people, but they showed love like they knew my ass.

Me and Poetry decided to take a break to eat something. There was so much food that I didn't know what to choose. So, I helped myself to a little bit of everything.

There was chicken, catfish, perch, tilapia, shrimp, Swedish meatballs, potato salad, cole slaw, spaghetti, rolls, macaroni salad, and even my favorite, lasagna. I found a seat at the table that was reserved for me and sat down. Dray came over and took a seat in the chair next to me.

"Are you enjoying yourself, beautiful?"

"I sure am! This is the best party ever all thanks go to you! Thank you again, Dray," I said, kissing his lips. "Did you eat yet?"

"Nah, but I will. I just wanted to make sure that you were all right over here. Um, there's someone that wants to meet you. Do you mind if I send him over?"

Him? I thought to myself. I was confused as to who *him* was. I didn't know what to say right away, so I kept eating. I ate a little bit more before I answered him. "Let me finish eating because I'm starving, then whoever it is can come over," I said, popping a meatball in my mouth.

"Okay, I'll let him know. I'll be back," he said, getting up.

Poetry came to the table with two plates of food looking like she hadn't eaten in years. All I could do was look at the plates in awe because I was trying to figure out how she was going to eat it all. She had some things that I didn't get so I had plans to eat off her plate with her.

"What are you doing with all of that food, boo?" I asked when she sat down and got comfortable.

"Shid, I'm gon' eat it! What the hell you thought? I just came from outside smoking with Monty's ass. A bitch got the munchies," she said, biting into a piece of chicken.

"How the hell you end up outside when you were behind me at the food table?"

"Don't worry about all that. Eat your food, little grasshopper," she said, laughing.

Shaking my head at her, I went back to eating my food. I remembered what Dray said about someone wanting to meet me. I wanted to know if she knew anything about it. "Bestie, do you know about a man that wants to meet me?"

She started choking on the food that she had in her mouth. I hit her a couple times on the back and handed her a cup of water to wash whatever it was down. She grabbed a napkin to wipe her eyes and took a few deep breaths.

"You okay?" I asked her with concern.

"Yeah, I'm good. A piece of chicken tried to take a bitch out. But um, nawl. I don't' know anything about that. It could be anybody. There is a lot of people here to help you party. I don't know half of these muthafuckas, but your money case is stacked, boo. Your pockets gon' be straight for college. The way your dress was looking, I thought it was made out of money," she said, laughing.

I didn't know anything about a money case, but I would find out before I left the building. The letters on the wall along with my pic, were going to college with me. That shit was dope, I thought to myself as I looked at it. I finished eating then got up to throw the plate in the garbage. I stopped in my tracks when I heard the last voice I wanted to hear. Dot was in the building and she could be heard over the music.

"Who invited her?" I asked Poetry as I turned to face her.

"I have no clue. Everyone agreed that she was not to know about your party, Kaymee. I don't even know how she made it past security," she told me.

Before I could say anything, Dot was a few feet away from me. I couldn't move, my feet felt as if they were glued to the floor. I had no worries in the past couple weeks because I was away from her. The feeling of fear was present full force. When she spotted me at the table, she started yelling at me.

"Bitch, you thought you were about to be partying it up for your birthday without me. I'm still your muthafuckin' mama! I'm supposed to know everything that goes on with you. I haven't heard from your ass in weeks. It's time for you to bring your ass back home, bitch!"

She was so close in my face that our noses almost touched. I didn't know what she was so angry about. Any other time, she didn't want anything to do with me. But she wanted to clown because someone did something nice for my birthday and she wasn't invited. She needed to get the fuck on with the bullshit.

"You haven't celebrated my birthday since I was six, Dot. Who is you trying to front for? I'm never going back to live in your house. What you did to me was the last time you will ever treat me like shit again. I don't know how you found out about this party, but I want you to leave. Today is all about me and I don't want you to be part of it. So, you can see your way out or I will have you removed," I said, stepping back.

I knew she would try to swing on me. That's why I moved back. That didn't stop her from remaining in my face. With every step back I took, she took two forward. In my mind, I was wondering where Dray or Monty was. I knew she was going to try to fight me. I quickly glanced to look at Poetry, but she wasn't at the table anymore. I was pissed because she knew what Dot was capable of and she left me. I could feel the tears forming in my eyes. I didn't want them to, but I didn't have any control.

"You can tell me what you ain't doing, but I still have the right to tell you want you're gonna do, bitch. And I said you are coming back home! You are leaving this club with me right now!" she yelled, grabbing arm.

I snatched away from her and as soon as I did, she slapped the fuck out of me. I threw my hands up to shield my face and she started hitting me in my head with her fist. There were so many people around, but no one did anything. Once again, my mama was embarrassing me. I couldn't enjoy life because she didn't want me to.

She was fucking me up, but I couldn't fight back. I knew as soon as I lifted my head, she was going to go to work on my face. I wasn't trying to be a bloody mess at my party. That was her problem, she was jealous of me. Dot stopped hitting me suddenly, but I didn't know why until I heard a deep baritone bellow out, "Dorothy Morrison, I'll kill yo' muthafuckin' ass!"

Chapter 13
Montez

I was sitting at the bar in the back with G, Dray, and some of the other homies that came to support Kaymee. I hadn't seen these niggas in months. Scony's muthafuckin' ass was still crazy as hell but he had mellowed down since he'd gotten married and had a son. Conte was the newest nigga of the Goon Squad, but he's cool as fuck. I liked the nigga's drive. Tonio's ass was standing up looking like a damn body builder and shit, watching what was going on around us. The only one that was missing was that nigga Quan, but his ass didn't party much with his nerdy ass.

"Look at baby girl over there looking like a muthafuckin' beluga whale in that grey dress. She knew she was too big for that joint. Her friends need their ass whooped for letting her come outside like that. I bet when she asked them how she looked, they all said, 'Girl, you got it going on!', lying they ass off," Scony said loudly.

We all started laughing because the shit was funny. The way he imitated what her girls sounded like had my stomach hurting. That nigga didn't give a damn what he said out his mouth and he could care less about who heard him. I was taking a sip of my Corona when Poetry came running up. I saw the fear in her eyes as I jumped up immediately. I knew something was wrong because she didn't have any shoes on.

"Dot's here—"

That's all I heard before I grabbed her hand, letting her lead the way. When we got to the table where they were, there was a man that looked like a male version of Kaymee in Dot's face.

"Dorothy Morrison, I'll kill yo' muthafuckin' ass!" he bellowed out.

I didn't know who the fuck he was but he had to be family in some type of way. I looked at Kaymee and she

147

was crying. I rushed to her side, pulling her into my arms. Her body was shaking uncontrollably and I hated that shit. She was so afraid of her mama and it was a damn shame. I wanted to knock that bitch into the middle of next week. The deejay cut off the music and everything could be heard in that muthafucka.

"Fuck you, Jonathan! Where the fuck you been all her muthafuckin' life? I've been taking care of her, nigga! You ain't did shit for her with your deadbeat ass! Get the fuck outta my face, pussy!"

Dot was talking good shit to dude. That couldn't have been me though. I would've knocked her ass into the middle of next week talking crazy to me like that. I guess he heard my thoughts because he drew his hand back to knock fire from her ass, but G and Scony grabbed him.

"It ain't even worth it, Unc. The bitch ain't worth it," G said as he grabbed him and pushed him back. "Scony, get that bitch outta here before she come up missing!"

Scony grabbed Dot by her arm, trying to get her out of the club, but she wasn't having that shit. She was tussling with him, trying her best to get him to let her go. He flung her around to face him and through clenched teeth, he read her ass.

"I'm not Jonathan. I will fuck you up, bitch! Now, you are about to get your drunk ass out of here while you are still able to breathe on your own. You already know that I don't play with other people's kids. I will knock you the fuck out, Dot!"

She calmed down for a few but started right back up. She turned in Kaymee's direction, letting everyone see her stupid side. "I'm beating your ass every time I see you, bitch! You got lucky today, but it won't be the same results next time! Believe that shit! Just to let you know, that muthafucka don't give a fuck about you just like I don't. Where the fuck he been all your muthafuckin' life? You ain't never gon' be shit without me, bitch! Everything you try to be in life is gonna crumble at your feet! I'm gon' make your life a living hell, bitch!"

Scony had enough of her ass. He picked her up and slung her over his shoulder like a rag doll. But that didn't stop her from screaming and cursing. She was letting everything that was on her chest off before she was put out.

"Jonathan, I hope you can explain your absence to her simple ass. I hope she blames your ass for everything she's been through. After all, it's your fault for leaving my ass back in the day. You are the reason she got treated like shit, nigga! All you had to do was stay and love us, you bitch ass nigga! I loved yo' stupid ass but you ran, you coward! Fuck you, muthafucka!"

By that time, Scony had put her down outside and closed the door. Kaymee was still crying. Poetry came over and I stepped aside while she consoled her. She wiped her face with a napkin, whispering something to her that I couldn't pick up. Whatever she said, stopped the tears that flowed down Kaymee's face.

Dray came over and grabbed Kaymee, sitting her on his lap. He too was saying the right things to her because after a while, she had completely stopped crying and was laughing a little bit. My boy had it bad for her. I've never in two years saw him go all out for any female back in Atlanta. He put his all into making her birthday special and I had to give him his props. Even though he couldn't afford the shit, he still made it happen regardless of how it was paid for.

The shit that Dot said had me wondering what the fuck was really going on. I knew I wasn't the only one that picked up the fact that she called Jonathan a deadbeat, She said he wasn't there for eighteen years and he was the reason Mee went through the shit she went through. That shit didn't take a rocket scientist to figure out that nigga was Mee's daddy! And I was about to see why his muthafuckin' ass decided today was the day he wanted to show the fuck up.

I marched over to the corner that G had cleared to calm Jonathan down. G and Scony were over there with the nigga. They stopped talking when they saw me storming over. I didn't give a fuck what they were saying. I had some shit I wanted to say my damn self. G and Scony already knew how the fuck I was. They groomed me into the Goon I was today.

"Aye, Patna. I got a couple questions for you. Why the fuck you all of a sudden show up for Mee now?"

"Hold up, youngin'. Don't approach me like that if you don't know what the fuck you talking about!" Jonathan said, stepping to me.

This nigga must be out of his muthafuckin' mind walking up on me. I knew more than he did about Mee and that's his fuckin' daughter. I saw he was a hothead just like me, but that's the way I liked niggas to be. I wanted them to be able to match me toe to toe. I didn't waste my energy on weak niggas.

"Oh, I know what I'm talking about! Mee is like a little sister to me. I was the one that got her away from that psycho ass bitch. I almost took her muthafuckin' head off because she beat that girl so bad. Don't tell me I don't know what the fuck I'm talking about! I was the one checking up on her, making sure she was good in that muthafuckin' apartment! And I was doing the shit all the way from the A, my nigga. I made sure her cellphone bill was paid so she could call if she needed me. It was me that made sure she had clothes on her back and food in her stomach when that bitch wouldn't do shit. It was me that called my muthafuckin' cousin to get her a fuckin' job! I was the one that told her to go open a bank account and taught her how to save her money. It was me that told her enough was enough and she needed to leave! So, don't tell me I don't know what the fuck is going on! And by the expressions on y'all faces, nain one of you niggas knew what the fuck that bitch was doing to her!"

I had to say that shit because that nigga was under the impression that I was a clueless muthafucka. The only thing I was clueless about was where the fuck this nigga been all these years and why he chose now to show the fuck up. That's all I wanted to know at that point.

"Damn, youngin'. You right, I didn't know none of that shit was going on. You opened my eyes to a lot of shit and I think I should be thanking you. But I want to say this. Don't ever come at me the way you did a few minutes ago. I will kill yo' ass."

"If it has anything to do with Kaymee Shanice Morrison, I wouldn't change a muthafuckin' thing about how I came at you. Other than my woman, that's the only one I will kill for. If there is a next time I have to approach you in this manner, get ready to strap up. And don't forget yo' army 'cause you gon' need 'em. Go talk to your daughter because I'm quite sure she heard all the shit that bitch said just like I did. She deserves an explanation, I don't," I said, walking off from his ass.

I went to go find Mee to see if she was straight. I spotted her on the dance floor with Dray, so I knew she was in good hands. Poetry was sitting down at the table eating and I went to join her. I hadn't eaten all night and a nigga was starving. I made a beeline to the food table and stacked a plate. Going to the table with my baby, I kissed her on the cheek and sat down.

"Damn, baby. That shit was wild. How the fuck did Dot find out about the party?" she asked me before taking a sip of whatever she was drinking.

"I wish I knew! I wanted to beat her ass! The way she was acting, you would have thought Mee was fucking her man or some shit. That bitch need help for real."

"There were a couple people that thought that's exactly what it was about. I had to check they ass on that shit quick. Don't go starting no rumors about my damn girl. This ain't what that is. I had to talk to Kaymee because she thought I left her to deal with Dot alone. Shid, I knew to come get you."

"You did the right thing by coming to get me, but when it comes to Dot don't leave her alone. We all know that Dot is always trying to break her down, and she does that by putting her hands on her. It's a good thing she didn't do that shit tonight," I said, biting into my chicken.

"She was fighting her, bae. That's why that dude said he would kill her. Kaymee told me when we were talking. She said Dot slapped her and punched her in her head several times. The only reason she stopped was because dude stopped her."

"I wish I would've known. I would've knocked her on her ass. I don't know why she showed up anyway. What was the muthafuckin' point? It's like she wants that damn girl to fail so she would have to come back to her. I would never let that shit happen, even if I have to foot every one of her bills. I'll handle it."

Poetry stopped eating and wiped her hands on a napkin. "Montez, is that dude Kaymee's daddy? That's what I gathered from the things Dot was yelling out," she asked, staring at me.

"Yeah, that's her dad. Don't say anything to Mee about it. I'm quite sure she put two and two together already. He will be talking to her before the night is over. I already had a talk with him."

"I think we should bring out the cake. That would put a bigger smile on her face. What do you think?" Poetry asked, finishing her drink.

"That's a good idea. Let me fuck this food up first. I have to honor my sis on the mic before that part takes place. You know how I do. In the meantime, you can go to the kitchen and roll out the cake. I'll text one of these niggas to help you," he said with a smile on his face.

***

When I finished eating, I went to the bathroom to wash my hands. That food hit the spot. Now, I was ready to get my drink on. I made my way to the deejay booth and grabbed the mic. He turned the music down and all heads turned in our direction. I noticed that Poe did what I asked her to do and that meant it was time.

"I want to thank everyone for coming out to make this day special for my sis. Kaymee, come over here baby girl."

Watching her walked over to the booth, she looked beautiful. When she stepped onto the stage, I couldn't stop smiling. My sis was shittin' on these hoes and didn't even know it. She was holding her head down. I knew it was because of the stunt her mammy pulled. I had something in store for her that was going to make her dance a jig. I pulled her close and held the mic to my mouth.

"I've known this woman for the past four years and she has grown tremendously. Not just in size, but in maturity, academics, and as a person in general. She is the coolest person you could ever meet. If she could, she would give you the shirt off her back. That's why I love her with everything in me. The shit y'all witnessed earlier, don't try to figure that shit out. What it looked like ain't what it is. Now, we gon' leave it alone."

I glanced down at Mee and she still had her head down. I bent down and whispered in her ear, "Hold your head up. This is your day. Don't ever let anyone blow your light out. You were meant to shine and I want you to shine brighter than the diamonds that's resting on top of your head. Ya feel me?"

She shook her head yes, then I continued what I was saying. "Kaymee is gonna go far in life and I'm gonna make sure she does. I don't want her to have to worry about finances or anything else for that matter. She has a full ride to Spelman, paid in full. She has her own money saved up from working but how long will that last? As a big brother that likes to do big thangs, who got the most trustworthy muthafuckas on his team that's willing to pitch in, I want to present something to you, Mee." I reached behind me and pulled out cardboard check.

"I want you to be able to go away to school without a care in the world even though I will be right by your side. I am honored to present this check, for—none of y'all damn business!" That got a laugh out of everyone. "Nah, for real. I want you to have this check. The money is already in an account and I'll give you everything associated with it. Don't kill me when you see the dollar amount, okay? I love you, sis. Keep rising to the top," I said, kissing her cheek.

The applause was loud as hell in the building and I was happy for her. The smile I was waiting for finally appeared. It got even bigger when Dray stepped on stage. He grabbed her in a hug and kissed her lips passionately. He was holding a long jewelry box and she started shaking her head no. She snatched the microphone from me and held it behind her back. Turning toward her guests, she took a deep breath.

"I would like to thank all of you for coming out. I appreciate all the gifts that I received and y'all coming out. I don't know half of y'all, but I feel the love all the same. It's been years since I've celebrated my birthday. Y'all don't know what y'all done with this day. Poetry, I love you girl for always being the best sister and friend to me. I wouldn't trade you for the world."

"I love you back, bestie!" Poe yelled out from the crowd.

"Monty, I love you bro for always being there to save me. I don't know where I would be if it wasn't for you. I'm forever indebted to you." I shook my head no repeatedly, but she couldn't see me. Everyone else did though. "Dray, thank you for putting this together with the help of my two best friends, and anyone else that had a hand in this surprise. When I first met you, I liked you from the gate, but you screamed playa and I didn't want that. But the way you've been there for me the past month and a half, I can no longer ignore it. You have made me smile when I didn't want to. I know for a fact you would have nursed my wounds had you known. I want to tell you in front of everyone tonight, that I choose you."

"I choose you too, baby," Dray said, kissing her again before he stepped back.

"I want to thank you all again for coming out. Enjoy the rest of the night with me. Let's party," she said, handing me the mic.

"Hold on! It's time to sing happy birthday! Bring out the cake!" I yelled into the mic.

At that moment, Tonio rolled the cake to the middle of the floor. I put the mic down and made my way to the floor. The cake we decided to have made was shaped into the number eighteen with editable pics of Mee with Poetry, Dray, and me. However, majority of the pictures were of Mee. The designs of the cake were the colors of the decorations and the candles were eighteen long-stemmed candles. Kaymee's smiled when she saw it, so I knew that she loved it.

The workers at the club were already cleaning up, so I knew we didn't have much longer to party. I looked down at my watch and it was three fifteen in the morning. We had forty-five minutes before the club closed. I pulled out my phone and texted G so he could start helping us move her gifts and shit to the cars.

The deejay started the music to the Stevie Wonder's version of happy birthday, the entire building sang loudly. Mee was blushing and rocking back and forth with a huge smile on her face. When she blew the candles out, the deejay switched the track to R Kelly's, "Happy birthday". The cake was moved by the food and the party started right back up.

Mee and Poe were in the center of the dance floor dancing to the song. Money was flying in the air falling to their feet. The deejay made it clear to everyone on the dance floor when he announced, "All the money that's on the floor stays on the floor. Don't touch that shit!"

I started laughing my ass off because he was serious. I wanted Mee to open her gifts, but there were too many of them muthafuckas for real. We would have to sit with her later while she opened them because it wasn't happening. We had about another thirty minutes before it was time to head out, and I wanted Mee to enjoy every minute of it.

After a while, it was four o'clock and the party was officially over. Dray and I had already agreed that we were all going back to my place. I had already given one of the lil' nigga's my keys to the crib and all of Mee's gifts and shit was already there. The only items we had to take with us was her money case.

"You ready to roll out, ma?" I asked Poetry.

"Yeah, I'm tired as hell. This was the best party ever, drama and all," she said, laying her head on my shoulder. I couldn't agree with her more.

I saw Dray by the door hugged up with Mee, so I walked towards them. She looked sleepy and she had every reason to be. She had her shoes and purse in her hand. Dray said something to her and she shook her head no and laughed. Out the corner of my eye, I saw Jonathan walking across the floor in her direction. I knew then the truth was about to be told.

Chapter 14
Kaymee

I was enjoying the alone time with Dray without all the music booming in my ear. My surprise party was one for the books and I really enjoyed myself. I couldn't get enough of Dray's kisses. His lips were so soft. The way he held me had me feeling secure in his arms. I was ready to go so I could take a shower and go to bed. I was exhausted.

The things that Dot had said earlier were on my mind, but I didn't want to bring it up to anyone. For the rest of the night, I wanted to find the mystery man that she screamed all of those hateful words to and ask him all the questions I had put together in my head. I knew I wasn't the only person that heard her call him a deadbeat, screaming out all of those questions at him.

I needed answers and he was the one that could give them to me. Dot wasn't going to tell me and if she did decide to talk about the situation, she was going to spew lies out of her mouth. I felt the Jonathan dude didn't have a reason to lie to me. From the looks of things, he looked like a straightforward person, but looks could be deceiving.

"What's on your mind, Kaymee?" Dray asked. "Are you thinking about taking my virginity tonight?"

What he said was funny as hell because he was far from a virgin. I threw my head back and laughed at him, while shaking my head no. That was the furthest thing on my mind. He had a better chance of getting the goodies earlier. My mind wasn't clouded by all of the surprises now, so he was shit out of luck.

"No, baby. We are on my time, remember? Or too much partying messed with your memory?"

Before he could answer my question, I heard someone walking up to us. I turned around and Jonathan was standing in front of me. Now that I could see his entire face, I could tell that he was a male version of me. Dot's words came back to the forefront of my mind when she said, *"You look just like your damn daddy. That's why I can't stand your ass."* He couldn't deny me at all.

"Hi," was all I could come up with to say.

"Hello, Kaymee. Can we talk for a little while, please?" he asked lowly.

Monty and Poetry were walking in our direction as it was time for us to leave the club. I really didn't know what to say to this man. He was a complete stranger to me. Even though I wanted to talk, it was past four in the morning and I just wanted to sleep.

"Look, I know that we need to talk but it's late. I just had the best birthday ever and I just want to go so I can get some sleep. Would it be possible for us to meet up later today? We are gonna need more than a couple minutes to figure this shit out."

I didn't let my eyes falter from his at any given time. It was like looking in the mirror without my locs. The shit was scary in a sense. We had the same everything, eyes, nose, lips, and even our ears. I already knew that he was my daddy. What I didn't know was why didn't he come for me.

"I understand. Put my number in your phone. You can call me when you are ready to meet up. I still have to give you your birthday present anyway."

I wanted to tell him to shove the gift up his ass, but that's not my character. I was going to hear him out by listening to his side of the story. There were always three sides. In this case, there was four. My side, his side, Dot's side, then there was the truth. Dot couldn't be trusted so I didn't give a damn what she had to say, but I knew she'd better stay far away from me. I wasn't taking anymore of her shit.

"Sure, I can do that," I said, taking my phone out of my purse.

I unlocked my phone and handed it to him so he could insert his number. Looking to my right, Monty and Poetry were still standing there while Dray was still behind me. I didn't mind them being there because again, I didn't know this man.

"Thank you for giving me an opportunity to get to know you and explain everything. I know eighteen years is a long time, but it wasn't that long. Still, it was a long time regardless. I will be waiting on your call, Kaymee," he said sadly.

"I will make sure to call, I promise. Dray, I'm ready to go now." I said heading to the door.

When I got outside, the tears started to fall but I checked that shit. I wasn't about to cry. I'd done enough of it. I had to stay strong for me. There would be no more breaking me down, using myself as a stepping-stone. That shit was over with. It was either come correct or don't come at all.

"Are you okay, babe?" Dray asked.

"Yes, I am," I replied, looking everywhere but at him.

Poetry came out of the club carrying my money case. Monty came out a few minutes later. We all got into Monty's truck, Poetry and me in the back, and the guys in the front. On the ride to the house, I laid my head on the window. I felt myself drifting off when Monty started talking to me.

"Mee, I want you to hear me out. Jonathan wants to talk to you about everything. Give him a chance to explain. Can you do that for me?"

"Monty, I already had it in my mind to talk to the man. It just wasn't gonna be at that time. I'm tired. I had a wonderful day and I just want to cuddle with my man and go to sleep. Is that alright with you?"

"Yeah, I hear what you are saying. The only thing I'm trying to say is direct your anger towards Dot's ass."

"And all I'm saying is drop this shit for now."

I laid my head back on the window and closed my eyes. Sleep was invading my thoughts and I didn't know how much longer I was going to be able to hold on. I didn't realize I fell asleep until I felt my body being picked up. I opened my eyes wide enough to see we were at Monty's place. Then they closed automatically.

The wetness that was on my face jolted me from my sleep. I looked up and Dray was sitting on the side of the bed with a towel in his hand. I smiled and sat up. "I think I can finish what you started. Thank you for trying but this makeup has to come completely off. Can I get up please?"

Dray got up and I walked to the door, going down the hall to the bathroom. The sound of Poetry and Monty's moans and groans could be heard as if they were connected to a speaker. I didn't understand how they had the strength to be in there fucking like rabbits after the night we had. I went in the bathroom and turned on the water. I didn't have any of my facial cleansers with me, so warm water would have to do.

I cleaned my face as best as I could then turned on the shower. I needed to wash the residue of sweat from my body. As much as I wanted to sleep, I couldn't go to bed without washing. I took off my clothes and stepped into the shower. The water hit every part of my body except my hair, all of my worries washed down the drain. I washed my body twice and got out. Taking a clean towel from the linen closet, I dried off thoroughly and wrapped the towel around myself.

Picking my dress up from the floor, I left out of the steam-filled bathroom and walked back to the room that Dray occupied. He was laying in the bed wide awake, waiting on me to come back. I got into the bed with the towel still wrapped around me and laid down. I pulled the covers up to my neck and took the towel off, placing it on the chair that was by the bed.

"Did you enjoy your shower?" he asked, kissing my cheek.

"Yes, it was much needed. Now I can go to sleep. Would you close the curtains, please? The sun will be too bright soon and I would never fall asleep if they stayed that way."

He got up and did what I asked. I turned over and closed my eyes. The mattress dipped slightly when he got back into the bed but I didn't feel him next to me. Instead, I felt the cool breeze from the air conditioner, hitting the bottom of my feet. I didn't think anything of it until I felt something wet against my thigh.

The movement continued upward toward my love box and at that point, I was afraid to open my eyes. My body was turned so that I was lying on my back. Still, I couldn't open my eyes. I knew what was about to happen and I wanted it to, but I knew that I should stop it. I opened my mouth to protest, but at the same moment, Dray had inserted his tongue in my tunnel.

My back arched off the bed and I felt like I was elevating into the air. Poetry always talked about the feeling of being eaten out, but I didn't imagine the feeling being like that. My legs voluntarily opened on their own, my hands finding the back of his head. That was his green light to continue what he was doing.

A low moan escaped my lips and I felt a tingling sensation in the pit of my stomach. I laid there not knowing what to do, I started feeling self-conscious. Instead of holding his head against my pussy, I pushed it away. The popping sound of my clit being released from his mouth, sounded so sensual and it felt good, too.

"What's wrong, baby? You didn't like it?" Dray asked, coming from under the covers.

"Actually, I loved it but I don't think I'm ready to do that," I said in a breathy voice.

"I won't force you to do anything else. Just let me please you, baby. You taste so good," he said, kissing my inner thigh once more.

The tingling feeling was back full throttle. I knew my bud was about to have a mind of its own. My mind said no, but my lower regime was singing a different tune. I wasn't fighting, so he wasn't backing up. He continued to tease my second set of lips and I liked it. When he French-kissed them, I almost yelled out.

My hands found his head again and held it in that position. His lips wrapped around my clit and he sucked softly at first. Then he sucked it harder. It hurt so good, I didn't want him to stop. I moaned loudly and I grabbed the pillow, putting it over my face.

"Oh shit, Dray!" I moaned into the pillow.

He was eating my pussy so good, I couldn't think straight. He did all types of tricks with his tongue and it was making my toes curl. There was a feeling in my stomach that I only felt when I had to pee. I didn't want to pee in this man's mouth. That was nasty. I threw the pillow to the side so he could hear my words clearly.

"Dray, Dray, Dray—" I couldn't get the rest of the words out because this man was sucking my soul from my body. Still, I had to tell him I had to pee. If I didn't, he would hate me forever. "Baby, you gotta—you gotta move. I got to go to the bathroom, Dray. I gotta pee! Please, let me up! I don't want to pee in your mouth."

It didn't matter what I said or how loud I said it. He wouldn't stop sucking on my clit. I tried pushing his head away but it felt as if he was pushing it forward just as hard. He had a death grip on my clit and I didn't believe he had any intentions of letting it go. The urge to pee was even stronger than before and I was trying to hold it in. With every breath that I took, the urge got stronger. The tears that were burning my eyes, slid down the side of my face soaking the sheet under my head.

"Please let me go to the bathroom, Dray! It's about to come out!"

"Let that shit go. It's not pee. It's my potassium and I want it," he said, burying his head back in my snatch.

He went in harder than before, moving his head from side to side. He continued to suck hard, sticking his finger into my opening. I flinched a little bit, because nothing had ever been in that hole. It hurt but only for a second once the sensation moved from my stomach to my kitty, overpowering it.

Dray continued to use his finger to penetrate me, while his mouth worked overtime. At that point, the friction was unbearable and I couldn't hold off anymore. I took another deep breath then I felt the fluid shooting out like a broken faucet.

"Oh my God! What are you doing to me!" I screamed, while holding his head between my legs. "Shit! Damn! Fuck! Yasssssss, Dray! Uggggggggh!"

I had never screamed like that a day in my life. The feeling felt as if it would never go away as it subsided little by little. Then all of a sudden, it was over. I couldn't move and the ringing in my ears was loud. My breathing was labored and my kitty was sore. I couldn't hold my eyes open and before I knew it, everything turned black.

***

The words, *"You were the reason she got treated like shit, Jonathan!"* kept playing over and over in my head like a broken record. I was trying to get away from them but they kept echoing in my head louder and louder. I saw the look on her face when she screamed them, seeing all the hurt. But I didn't feel sorry for her. I couldn't have any pity because she never had any for me.

I was finally able to open my eyes and the first thing I did was scan the bed. I breathed a sigh of relief because outside of the scene at the club with Dot, I had another dream about Dray putting his mouth on me. I knew I had to be dreaming to think about that happening. That would've only led to sex, which was something that I wasn't ready for at all.

I pulled the covers over my body because some time or another, I came from under them. It was cold as hell and I wanted to text Monty or Poetry to tell them to turn that shit down a little bit. In order to do that, I would have to get up but that wasn't in the plans. As I turned over, I felt something wet on my thigh. I moved the cover and lo and behold, there was a big wet spot under my ass and it went as far as my lower thigh.

Sitting there, I wondered if I had actually pissed on myself like I recalled screaming in my dream. I jumped up in a panic and there was a slight pain between my legs. It wasn't "My hole" that was hurting, it was solely in the clit area. I looked down and pulled my lower lips upward and my clit was bigger than usual. I touched it and flinched. It was tender to the touch.

I stood on the side of the bed looking stupid as fuck. I was fighting to remember what I did when I got in earlier that morning, but I couldn't remember. The only thing that came to mind was the dream that I had. I was so confused and a little scared. I didn't know how a dream would make my clit hurt in real life.

Inspecting the wet spot, I leaned down and sniffed the sheet. It didn't smell like pee at all, but I could clearly see that it was still somewhat wet. My mind wouldn't let me be great by helping me figure this shit out. This was not the time to play riddle me by my damn self.

The sound of the door opening had me diving in bed and jumping under the covers. Dray came in carrying a tray of food with one of my roses in a glass of water. He had on a pair of basketball shorts and a tank top. Seeing him without a full shirt on had my mouth watering. Following his every move, I couldn't take my eyes off him.

"Good afternoon, beautiful. I made you some breakfast. Did you sleep well?" he asked, sitting the tray on the nightstand on my side of the bed.

"Good afternoon," I said, twisting the sheet between my fingers. "I slept fine, I think."

I wasn't able to look him in his eyes. Somewhere in the back of my mind, there was a voice telling me that I pissed in the bed. This shit was embarrassing. I had never pissed in the bed and now when I was with a man, it happened.

"What do you mean by that?" he asked, lifting his leg to get in the bed.

"No! Don't get in this bed, Dray!"

He paused abruptly and looked at me strangely. I couldn't let him get in a wet ass bed. I didn't know how I was about to explain this. He lowered his leg and kept his hands planted on the bed. I could feel him looking at me but I couldn't face him.

"Kaymee, what's the problem? You looked spooked over there. Did I do something wrong?" he asked softly.

"This is so embarrassing. I woke up from a dream and, and, the bed is wet. I think I peed on myself," I mumbled the last part.

"What about the wet spot? I didn't catch the last part," he said with a little bit of humor in his voice. I didn't want to repeat that shit, but it was only right that I did.

"I think I pissed in the bed, okay!" I screamed at him.

He started laughing and it only angered me. I couldn't believe that he thought my grown ass pissing in the bed was funny. I whipped my head in his direction, wanting to slap the shit out of him. He literally had tears running down his face as he held his stomach. It wasn't that funny. In fact, it wasn't a laughing matter.

"How the fuck do you find this funny, Drayton? This is embarrassing as hell!" I said, jumping up and snatching the linen off the bed.

"Kaymee, stop!" he said, continuing to laugh.

"What, Dray?" I yelled, throwing the sheet on the floor.

He looked at me like I shot his mama in the pinky toe or something. He went to the dresser and grabbed one of his shirts out of the drawer, holding it out to me. I snatched it and put it on before grabbing a pillow to take the case off. I was hotter than fish grease because he laughed at my mishap. If anything, he was supposed to make me feel better about what had happened.

"You did not pee on yourself, babe. You don't remember giving me permission to show you what this mouth do?" he asked with a smirk on his face.

I was horrified by what he said. I took a minute to process his words. All this time I thought I dreamt that incident and it really happened. Then I was running around this room because I thought I had wet the bed. I felt my face getting hot and I didn't know what to say, so I kept fumbling with the pillowcases.

"I don't think you want to face the fact that my tongue was deep inside your wetness, and boy did it get wet," he said, walking around the bed. "That pussy tasted good, too. Better than a Georgia peach. You definitely quenched my thirst. I'm glad you kept all of that greatness bottled up for me. It's real tight."

He stood in front of me licking his lips while looking at me lustfully. Taking me by the arm, he pulled me close. I buried my head in his chest so he couldn't see the look of shame on my face. Wrapping my hands around his waist, I tried to see the scene in my mind, but it wasn't there.

"You mean to tell me I'm not a virgin anymore and I don't even know what happened?" I whined into his chest.

"You are definitely still pure, baby. Things didn't go that far. It would've been nice, but I didn't take it there without your consent. There's nothing to be ashamed of, Kaymee. What we experienced last night was beautiful and we both enjoyed it."

I was an eighteen-year-old that wasn't told anything about what to expect when it came to sex. There weren't any talks about contraceptives, foreplay, first base, second base, none of that shit. The things Poetry tried to tell me didn't count because I couldn't stomach the nasty shit she said she had done. That was Dot's job to educate me on everything I needed to know. I wasn't surprised she didn't because I learned what a menstrual cycle was from the school nurse at ten.

"If there wasn't any penetration, how do you know what it feels like down there?" I asked, stepping back from him.

"I stuck my finger in and your walls closed around it tight as fuck! So, I know it's gon' do me right." He stood there shaking his head slowly.

"I need you to make me a promise. Let me initiate the sexual encounters from now on. Can you do that for me?"

He stood in front of me with his hand under his chin as if he was in deep thought. Then he looked down at me with a sneaky grin on his face. "Yeah, baby. About that, that's a promise I won't be able to keep. You already gave a nigga the opportunity to taste it. Ain't no turning back from that."

I didn't say anything to him. I just turned around and walked away.

***

Dray really pissed me off laughing at my dilemma. I was happy when he told me that we didn't physically have sex. I was so scared that he was going to say that we went all the way. But since that was cleared up and he basically told me that he wasn't going to let me initiate things, I was done talking to him.

167

I was looking around trying to figure out what I would wear for the day. I didn't have anything other than the dress I wore the night before. Staying out all night was not in my plans. I wasn't prepared for that day.

"I don't have any clothes here, Dray! I'm supposed to go out with Jonathan today."

"It's a good thing that ya girl looked out for you, huh? I brought your bag in this morning. It's over by the closet," he said, climbing back into the bed.

I walked to the closet and lo and behold, my black backpack was sitting on the floor. I picked it up and carried it to the bed. Inside, Poetry packed several outfits for me as well as sandals and under garments. Choosing a pair of black skinny jeans, a black tank top, and my coach flip-flops, I gathered everything in my arms and grabbed my phone.

"I'm going to shower. I'll be back."

"Okay, I'll be here when you get back," he said without taking his eyes off the TV.

Opening the door to go to the bathroom, I peeked into the living room as I walked. There were wrapped gifts sitting high by the door. I didn't recall seeing them when we came in the night before. Then again, I didn't remember much of anything when I got here. The sight of all the gifts made me giddy inside. I felt the love.

I couldn't take my eyes off the gifts. As I kept walking, I ran into somebody and I fell on my ass. I looked up and Poetry was standing over me laughing. She held her hand out to help me up. I reached up, allowing her to help me to my feet.

"Kaymee, what were you looking at?"

"It sure wasn't your strong body ass! Why didn't you say something? If you had, I wouldn't have ended up on the damn floor. I can't stand you sometimes," I said, walking around her.

I was at the bathroom door when she said, "Dray had that ass screaming, huh?"

I froze like I was doing the mannequin challenge. I couldn't believe she heard that shit. I was already embarrassed in front of him, now I was humiliated. I couldn't find the words to say and I couldn't move either.

"What's the matter, cat got your tongue?" she asked, laughing.

"Fuck you, Poetry!" was all I could say as I rushed into the bathroom and slammed the door.

Poetry was laughing from her gut outside the door and I wanted to go back out and cuss her out, but I couldn't face her. As I took off my clothes, she started knocking on the door trying to get in. I wasn't letting her ass in there with me. *Fuck her* is what the voice in my head kept repeating.

"Bestie, open the door!" she demanded, twisting the doorknob.

"Poetry get yo' ass off that damn door! Leave her alone! You were not supposed to throw that shit in her face like that! Get yo' ass in here," Monty yelled at her.

I couldn't do anything but laugh briefly, but all that shit stopped when I realized he heard the shit, as well. This was not supposed to happen to me! I started thinking to myself, how I was going to be able to face them after this shit. The thoughts were going crazy in my head as I turned on the shower. As the water warmed up, I took that time to send Jonathan a text.

Picking up my phone, I went to my contacts and found his number. My finger loomed over his name for a couple minutes before I pressed it. It took just as long for me to even start typing out the text. I finally said fuck it, starting the conversation.

Me: Good afternoon, Jonathan, this is Kaymee.

I went to the linen closet to get some clean towels and as I reached in, my phone chimed. He texted back quickly. I grabbed the towels, sat them on the sink, and picked my phone up again. I was kind of anxious to see what he had to say.

Jonathan: Hey, baby girl. I was wondering when I would hear from u. I thought u wasn't gon' reach out to me. What's going on?

Me: I wanted to know if we could have that sit down today. There's so many questions that I need answers to and there's no better time than now. I want to know the answer to one question in particular right now. Would you answer it truthfully?

I didn't waste any time responding back to his text. Meeting up with him as soon as possible was what I needed to do. There was no reason to prolong something that had already been put off for eighteen years of my life. Dot never told me a single thing about my daddy. He was not a subject that came up unless she was mad. That's when she started dogging him like he was shit.

Taking my clothes off, I was about to step in the shower when I received another text. I grabbed my phone and read what he had to say.

Jonathan: I am free to hang out with you. I can come pick you up if you like. As far as your other question, I think it would be better for me to answer any questions face to face.

Me: I don't have a car, so that will be fine. I want it to be just the two of us, so you can pick me up. 337 W. North Avenue. I'll be ready when you get here.

Jonathan: Okay, I got it.

I jumped in the shower and washed my body thoroughly. I didn't think to wrap my hair, so my locks were wet a little. It was in a bun, so it would be okay. Stepping out, I wrapped myself in a towel and brushed my teeth. It was still kind of warm out according to the weather app on my phone, so I wasn't bothering with makeup.

As I dried off my body, my stomach started to growl. I remembered Dray brought me food on a tray that I didn't touch. That was over an hour or so ago and I knew it was cold. It didn't matter, I would suggest getting something to eat with Jonathan. Hurrying to put on my clothes, I looked okay for a down day. I hung the towels on the rack and grabbed the t-shirt that I had earlier from the floor.

When I entered the bedroom, Dray wasn't in there. I put my phone in my back pocket, looking around to see what else I needed. Opening the purse that I had the night before, I took the money out and stuck it in my front pocket along with my ID. At that point, I heard voices coming from somewhere in the house.

I left out of the bedroom and followed the voices. Entering the living room, everyone was sitting down and having a conversation. Poetry was sitting on Monty's lap in the armchair, Dray was sitting on the loveseat, and Jonathan was sitting on the sofa. The conversation ceased when they noticed I was in the room.

"Y'all didn't have to stop talking. I'm a big girl. I can handle whatever it is," I said, looking around the room. No one said a word and I didn't force them to either. I walked over to Dray and kissed him on his lips. "I'll call you to let you know I'm okay. You need anything while I'm out?" I asked.

"Nah, just go and enjoy your day out. When you come back, we can open your gifts since you haven't thought about doing it," he said, kissing me again.

I gave Poetry a hug before I hugged Monty. He whispered in my ear, "Remember what I told you. Hear him out, Mee. Have an open mind, sis. He deserves that much," he said before he let me go.

I stood tall and looked at Jonathan. "Hey," I said, waving at him. He stood and opened his arms wide and I walked around the coffee table right into them. After he released me, I stepped back. "We can leave whenever you're ready," I said, giving him a small smile.

"Well let's get out of here then. I'll catch y'all later. Nice to meet you, Poetry. It was a pleasure."

We walked to the door together and left. I was ready to hear about all these demons that were forced upon me. It had been long enough and I wanted to hear it all.

Chapter 15
Jonathan

After I received the text from Kaymee wanting to meet up with me, I wanted to jump for joy. I had been waiting fourteen years for this moment. Seeing her at her party all grown up, tears freely ran down my face. I hadn't seen her since she was about four years old. I caught a drug charge and did twelve years in the fed joint. They dragged that shit on forever and it was bullshit. When I got out, the first thing I did was went to Dot's mama's house. That was the last place I knew she was.

I arrived at the house and there was another family living there. I wondered why Mae's letters stopped coming. I found out the reason that day when I went to the neighbor's house next door. Sheila was Mae's best friend. She was always there whenever I went to see Kaymee. I got the surprise of my life when she answered the door.

I rang the doorbell and waited patiently for her to open the door. The shuffling of her feet could be heard through the door. When she saw me, her face lit up brightly, giving me the biggest smile. It warmed my heart knowing that she remembered me. She unlocked the screen door and held it open with her hip, with her arms outstretched.

"Oh my God! Boy, where you been? It's been a long time!" she said, squeezing me tightly.

I looked down at her with a smile of my own. "It's nice to see you, too, Miss Sheila. I got in a little bit of trouble, so I was away for twelve years," I said shaking my head.

"Well, come on in. I know you didn't come over here to see me. I was probably an afterthought," she said, laughing. "But I'm quite sure I can answer the questions that I know will come my way. Have a seat," she said, motioning to the sofa.

Her house still looked the same from back in the day, nothing changed at all. She still had the same floor model television that we thought was the shit back then. And the plastic on her furniture was still in mint condition. The walls were a little yellow from the smoke that stuck to them. Sheila was never without her Benson and Hedges cigarettes.

"How have you been? You alright in here by yourself?" I asked her.

"Yeah, I'm alright. I won't complain., My God is good, baby," she said, reaching for her mug of coffee.

"When did Mae move, Miss Sheila?" I asked her softly.

The light went out of her eyes when I mentioned Mae. She took a deep breath and reached for her cigarettes. Taking one from the pack, she lit it and took a long drag. It seemed like she was having a hard time finding her voice. We sat there silently until she finished her cigarette. Putting it out and lighting another, she began to speak.

"Mae moved on to her eternal home, April 3, 1997. She had a heart attack and died upon arrival to the hospital. Little Kaymee was the one that found her and called the ambulance. I was so proud of that baby, she did what she was supposed to do. I miss that child so much. I haven't seen her since Dot took her away from here. Do you know that bitch didn't go to her own mother's funeral? That's why her siblings don't' have anything to do with her. She tried her best to get her oldest sister to take that child because she didn't want to raise her,." she said, dumping the ash from the cigarette.

I couldn't believe that Mae died. She didn't like the fact that I left Dot when she was pregnant, but I was right there when she had my baby. I stepped up to the plate and did what I had to do as a father. It wasn't on me that Dot refused to let me see my daughter. I didn't even know where she lived. She was spiteful because I wanted to see my daughter and not her.

The only time I was able to see Kaymee was when she was at Mae's house. I wanted to take my baby with me but Mae wasn't having it because of my lifestyle. She never turned me away when I came to her house to see her. I always brought something for her whenever I came over and left Mae with more than enough money to provide for her. Thinking about it now, I still made sure money was sent the entire time I was locked up.

"Sheila, do you know who took over Mae's mail after she passed?" I needed to know if my money was still going toward my baby's wellbeing.

"Dot got all the mail, forwarding the address to her place. I don't know where she is, though. I haven't seen her either," she said, rocking back and forth.

Sheila told me what I wanted to know. Even though she was not able to lead me to my daughter, I was glad to know she didn't end up in the foster care system. I sat and talked with her for a while before I made my way out the door, promising to check on her every now and again. Miss Sheila died a year later and it hurt me to my core. I paid to lay her to rest because she had no one else.

I shook my head a couple times to clear the memory. I got out of the truck and walked up the steps to the address Kaymee texted me. I press the doorbell and waited. The lil' nigga Monty answered.

"What up, man?" he said, stepping back so I could enter.

"Nothing much. I'm excited to see my daughter, that's about all," I said, waiting for him to lead the way to wherever I would wait.

"Mee is still getting ready. We can sit in the living room."

I followed him into the living room, Dray and the female I saw with Kaymee the night before was already seated. When Monty sat down, she stood and sat in his lap.

The way that lil' nigga came at me, I thought he had a thing with my daughter. There's one that thing I can say about him, though. The nigga had heart. He wasn't backing down for shit when he approached me.

"Aye Jay, man. Can you explain to me why you all of a sudden wanna get to know Mee after all of this time? I mean she don't even know you, dog," he said staring me directly in the eye.

"The reason I will talk to you about this before her is because I can tell you genuinely care about her. To answer your question, I've been searching for Kaymee. The last time I'd seen her was when she was four years old, I was locked up in the fed joint. I got out two years ago and that's when I learned that her grandmother had passed away. The lady that lived next door to them told me somethings, but the information didn't lead me to my daughter. No one knew where Dot was," I explained to him.

"How the fuck is that when G knew about her? That's ya muthafuckin' nephew!"

This nigga was on his gangsta shit and I was gonna let him have that. This wasn't the time for me to match his hostility.

"I live in Atlanta, my nigga. When I couldn't find my daughter, I left to take care of business down there. I will be the muthafucka you report to once you get back down there. Anyway, when y'all went to him about the party and he heard the name, how many Kaymee's do you know? I've never heard another female with that name. G hit me up and told me that he thinks he found my daughter. He told me all about the party and I was on the first thing smokin' to this muthafucka. When I saw her that night, it was like looking in a mirror. There was no denying it. Shit was confirmed when Dot came in showing her ass," I was saying when I heard footsteps.

My baby girl walked in the room and you could hear a mouse piss on cotton. She said her goodbyes to everyone then she finally spoke to me. I didn't see an ounce of her mama in her, that was all me. It was like I spit her out myself. She was finally ready to get the day started with me and I didn't want to waste another minute.

***

I let her walk out the door first and I followed behind her. I was almost to the truck when Monty called me back to the door. I climbed the steps to see what he wanted. He had a hard expression on his face. I stood there without saying anything, waiting to hear the lil' nigga out.

"Jay, she been through a lot already. Don't hurt her, man. If you're not in it for the long haul, move the fuck around now. She got one fucked up ass parent in her life. She don't need another one."

All I could do was respect what he had said. "I feel ya youngin' and I hear what you saying. I didn't wait all these years to disappoint her. She will always be heart. Last night was the first day that I felt that muthafucka beat the way it was made to do. I died on the inside looking for my baby. Not knowing where she was turned my ass into a cold-blooded nigga. Seeing her is melting that shit a bit. That's the only reason yo' ass didn't feel my wrath when you were on me with that Nino Brown shit," I said, patting him on the shoulder as I laughed. "I got her, man. That's my word."

Walking to the car, I hit the unlock button on the key fob. I walked to the passenger door so she could get in. Once she was seated, I closed the door and made my way to the driver's side. I sat there for a minute before starting up the truck. I kept stealing glances at her, taking in all of her beauty. She had locs and they were nice and neat, her light skin matched mine perfectly. I didn't realize I was smiling until she started laughing.

"Jonathan, are we going to leave the driveway anytime soon? A girl wanna eat," she said, continuing to laugh at me.

"Oh yeah, my bad. Where do you want to go? The choice is yours," I said, backing out of the driveway.

"Let's go to Olive Garden. I want lasagna."

"You got it, Garfield," I said to her as I headed to the expressway.

I saw her staring at me out the corner of my eye as I merged into traffic. "Speak your mind, baby girl."

She was quiet for a few seconds, fumbling with her phone. She looked out the window with a blank expression on her face. I wanted to push her to talk to me but I knew I couldn't do that. I had to give her the space to open up on her own. So, I continued to drive. It felt like forever when she finally broke the silence.

"I remember being called Garfield when I was younger. I never knew where it came from. Garfield is my favorite cartoon character." She paused again and I didn't interrupt her thoughts. "I always asked Grandma Mae to cook lasagna when I found out what the delicious dish was. Jonathan, are you my dad?" she asked with tears welling up in her eyes.

I got caught at the stoplight. It gave me the opportunity to glance over at her. The sadness displayed on her face tugged at my heart. The last thing I wanted her to do was cry. I knew when I revealed the truth, that's what she would do. It was my job to ease her mind that I wouldn't hurt her again.

"Yes, I'm your dad," I said, pulling off from the light. I hit the expressway and waited on her to say something. When she didn't, I continued to speak. "Kaymee, it wasn't my intention to be out of your life. I'm not gon' place the blame on anyone. All I can do is tell you my side of the story. I'm not gon' talk to you about anyone but myself. I did somethings in my life that I'm not proud of and I ended up being sent away for a very long time. I couldn't take you where I was, baby. I was in prison. Don't think for a minute that I didn't want to take you with me before that time because I did, because of my lifestyle, your Grandma Mae didn't allow you to live with me. I came to see you every day and I provided for you the entire time."

I exited the expressway. After driving a couple blocks, I pulled into the parking lot of the restaurant. Finding a parking space, I put the truck in park, unbuckling my seatbelt. Turning to face her, I watched her looking out the window. I reached over and turned her head in my direction.

"I never stop loving you, Kaymee. There wasn't a day that went by that I didn't think about you. Even while I was on lock, I provided for you. I sent money every month to take care of you up until I was released from jail two years ago." I reached over and hugged her, letting her get the cry out. "Come on, Garfield. Let's go eat some lasagna."

She smiled and wiped her eyes. I got out the truck and walked around to let my princess out. I hit the button to lock the doors and I grabbed her hand, leading the way into the restaurant. I requested a booth in the back away from everyone else. Once we were seated, the conversation continued.

"You mentioned that you sent money to take care of me for years, right?" she asked.

"Yes, I sent money faithfully every month. You were my responsibility, so it was my job to make sure you were well taken care of. Why do you ask?"

The waitress came over as I finished what I was saying to take our orders. I placed the order for Kaymee's lasagna and I ordered chicken alfredo. When she asked if we wanted anything to drink, we both said strawberry lemonade at the same time. We laughed, breaking the ice between us.

"Back to what we were talking about, I asked that question because I've never seen any of that money once I left Grandma Mae's. After she passed away, I moved with Dot. She didn't want me and she let it be known every day. I cried all the time when I got to her house because I never saw my grandma again and Dot was never at home. I basically raised myself from the age of six. If my grandma hadn't taught me how to take care of myself, I would've been fucked up. I knew nothing about you, not even your name. All I knew was you were a sorry muthafucka and I looked just like you. I got a job at sixteen so I wouldn't starve and to buy clothes and toiletries. She tried her best to take damn near my whole check every two weeks. If I didn't have Monty and Poetry in my life, I don't know where I would be today. Living with that woman was hell," she said, taking a sip of water.

My heart was breaking with every word that came out of her mouth. I never thought Dot would take the hatred that she had for me out on our daughter. To hear that her mother didn't give a fuck about her had me seeing red. I wanted to wring her muthafuckin' neck.

"A few weeks ago, she beat me so bad I had to go to the hospital. I didn't even tell the doctors that she was the one that did me like that. I know it might sound crazy, but I didn't want her to get in trouble," she said, looking down at the table.

"At least she had the decency to take you to the hospital. That was the least her dumb ass could do," I said, holding her hands.

She looked up at me, shaking her head no. I didn't know what she was trying to say. "She didn't take me to the hospital. One of her friends took me. She went in her room and laid down."

The tears flowed down her cheeks constantly. I got up and sat beside her, wrapping her in my arms. Her body was shaking so hard and her cries were muffled, she was trying not to draw attention to us. My heart was hurting because my baby was in pain from the things that Dot had done to her. For many years, I thought my baby was being taken care of. Instead, all that time, she was living her life in the worse way possible.

She stopped crying and I wiped her face with the cloth that was on the table. She looked up at me, forcing a smile. I kissed her on top of her head and held her close to my heart. I couldn't say anything at that moment because I was fighting back tears myself. The waitress was walking in our direction with our food.

"You ready to smash this shit, baby?"

"You remember how Garfield eats, right?" she asked, laughing.

I didn't bother moving back to the other side of the table. I wanted to be as close to my baby girl as possible as we sat enjoying the meal before us without any talking. We were killing that food for about five minutes then I decided to learn more about her. I didn't want to hear the sad shit anymore. I wanted to hear about her as a person.

"Tell me about Kaymee. I want to hear about you."

She ate a little bit more of her food then put her fork down and wiped her mouth. Turning around, she put her back against the wall, her face glowing out of nowhere. Sneaking another forkful of lasagna, once she swallowed what she had in her mouth, she cleared her throat.

"As you know, I'm eighteen and I graduated from high school in May. I was in the top of my class and I was accepted to eighty-three colleges. I chose to go to Spelman to study medicine. I want to be a neonatal nurse. I finished with a four-point three GPA and I did it all on my own," she said with so much pride.

"Wow, that's great! I wish I could've been there. I'm so proud of you, Kaymee."

"Thank you, Jonathan. You know I have pictures in my phone, right?" she said, grabbing her phone from the table.

As we continued to eat, she showed me the pictures from her graduation as well prom. She was so beautiful in every shot that I saw. I found myself telling her to send each one to me via text. I was having the proud daddy moment that I'd always dreamt of. I was happy to see her smiling, too.

"So why did you choose to go to Spellman?"

"I chose that college because it's a great school and also because Poetry will be there with me. Not to mention Monty is at Morehouse, and my now boyfriend goes there, too. They were the only family I had until you came back into my life, of course. I wanted to be where they were. I could've went anywhere, but I didn't want to be by myself."

"That's ironic that you would be in Atlanta. I live there Kaymee."

When I said that, she threw her arms around my neck, squealing loudly. I laughed while telling her to calm down. She finally let me go and looked at me funny. I didn't know where the change came from, but she wasn't looking too long.

"Wait a minute. Do I have siblings?" she asked, propping her chin on her fist.

I chuckled and shook my head no before saying the word out loud. "No, baby. I never had any more children. I didn't want to be the father to more children when I wasn't a father to you. Kaymee, you are my only child and I'm going to try my best to be the best father from this day forward. We can't go back in time. There's no way to make up those years, but the future holds a lifetime for us. We will make up for time lost. How does that sound?"

"I'm down with that, old man," she said, smiling.

"Do I look like a damn old man? You watch that shit!" I said, cutting my eye at her laughing.

The waitress came to our table with the check. Kaymee looked over my shoulder trying to see how much the bill was. I hid it with my hand and she stood up and went in her pocket. Turning her back on me, I could hear her rustling with money. I looked in her direction like she was crazy. I knew damn well she didn't think she was about to pay for the meal.

She tried to hand the waitress a hundred dollar bill and I pushed her hand down. "Baby girl, I got this."

She ignored me and stood on the seat, giving the waitress the money and had the nerve to say, "Keep the change." I couldn't do anything but shake my head.

"When I tell you I got it, that means I got it," I said to her sternly.

"Stop trippin', fool, I wanted to do something for you. Let me be great, old man," she said, smiling. "Man, that BMW truck is tight! That's you?"

I dug in my pocket pulling out the keys to the truck. I stared at them for a second before I answered her question. "It is tight, ain't it? You like it, huh?" I asked her.

"Hell yeah! I love it! The old man got good taste and it's a 2011 at that! You got it straight off the lot, didn't you? It looks brand new," she said, being nosy as hell.

"Yeah, it's brand new. I'm glad you like it because it's yours. Happy birthday, baby girl," I said, holding the keys out to her.

"Shut the front door! Stop playing with me, old man!" she screamed without taking the keys.

I lost count of how many times she hugged me that day, adding another one to them. She was choking the shit out of me and I loved every second I tried to catch my breath. Finally letting my neck go, she kept staring at the keys. Not one time did she try to take them from my outstretched hand.

"Will that truck still belong to me if I told you that I couldn't drive?" she asked me, laughing.

"Of course, it will. That only means that I have to teach you to drive that muthaucka. Let's get out of here, Garfield."

She hit me in my arm and followed it up with another hug. I felt like the luckiest man in the world. We were walking out the restaurant when I spotted Dot walking towards us with a dusty looking nigga. I grabbed Kaymee's hand and walked on to the truck, but we didn't make it halfway there before she saw us hand in hand.

"Ain't this a bitch! This nigga been missing all your muthafuckin' life and now he gets to play daddy! Bitch, I told you last night. Every time I saw you, I was gon' whoop yo' ass! I guess you thought I was playing," she said, walking in our direction.

"Dot, take that shit down a notch and gon' about yo' business. If you think I'm about to stand here while you try to fight my daughter, you must be crazy as hell. You better take yo' ass in there and feed that homeless nigga that you're with," I said, pushing Kaymee towards the truck.

The guy she was with was trying to hold her back, but she was pushing his ass away and punching him in the chest. I turned away to see if Kaymee got in the truck and before I knew it, she was running towards me.

"Go back to the truck, baby, I got this."

"Daddy, watch out!" she yelled, picking up speed to get to me.

Before she could make it to me, I heard a gunshot followed by a second one. An excruciating pain shot through my right side and I fell with a thud to the ground. I saw Dot and the dude running back in the same direction they came from. I was looking around for Kaymee but I didn't see her anywhere. I slowly turned over on my stomach. That's when I saw my baby girl lying motionless on the side of the truck.

To Be Continued...

**Love Shouldn't Hurt 2
Coming Soon**

Submission Guideline.

Submit the first three chapters of your completed manuscript to ldpsubmissions@gmail.com, subject line: Your book's title. The manuscript must be in a .doc file and sent as an attachment. Document should be in Times New Roman, double spaced and in size 12 font. Also, provide your synopsis and full contact information. If sending multiple submissions, they must each be in a separate email.

Have a story but no way to send it electronically? You can still submit to LDP/Ca$h Presents. Send in the first three chapters, written or typed, of your completed manuscript to:

LDP: Submissions Dept
Po Box 870494
Mesquite, Tx 75187

DO NOT send original manuscript. Must be a duplicate.

Provide your synopsis and a cover letter containing your full contact information.

Thanks for considering LDP and Ca$h Presents.

Coming Soon from Lock Down Publications/Ca$h Presents

BOW DOWN TO MY GANGSTA
By **Ca$h**
TORN BETWEEN TWO
By **Coffee**
BLOOD STAINS OF A SHOTTA **III**
By **Jamaica**
WHEN THE STREETS CLAP BACK **III**
By **Jibril Williams**
STEADY MOBBIN
By **Marcellus Allen**
BLOOD OF A BOSS **V**
By **Askari**
LOYAL TO THE GAME **IV**
By **T.J. & Jelissa**
A DOPEBOY'S PRAYER **II**
By **Eddie "Wolf" Lee**
IF LOVING YOU IS WRONG… **III**
LOVE ME EVEN WHEN IT HURTS
By **Jelissa**
DAUGHTERS OF A SAVAGE **II**
By **Chris Green**
TRAPHOUSE KING **II**
By **Hood Rich**
BLAST FOR ME **II**
RAISED AS A GOON **V**
By **Ghost**
ADDICTIED TO THE DRAMA **III**

By **Jamila Mathis**
LIPSTICK KILLAH **III**
By **Mimi**
WHAT BAD BITCHES DO **II**
By **Aryanna**
THE COST OF LOYALTY **II**
By **Kweli**
SHE FELL IN LOVE WITH A REAL ONE
By **Tamara Butler**
LOVE SHOULDN'T HURT II
By **Meesha**
CORRUPTED BY A GANGSTA **II**
By **Destiny Skai**
SHE FELL IN LOVE WITH A REAL ONE II
By **Tamara Butler**

Available Now
RESTRAINING ORDER **I & II**
By **CA$H & Coffee**
LOVE KNOWS NO BOUNDARIES **I II & III**
By **Coffee**
RAISED AS A GOON I, II, III & IV
BRED BY THE SLUMS I, II, III
BLAST FOR ME
By **Ghost**
LAY IT DOWN **I & II**
LAST OF A DYING BREED
BLOOD STAINS OF A SHOTTA I & II
By **Jamaica**

LOYAL TO THE GAME

LOYAL TO THE GAME II

LOYAL TO THE GAME III

By **TJ & Jelissa**

BLOODY COMMAS I & II

SKI MASK CARTEL I & II

By **T.J. Edwards**

IF LOVING HIM IS WRONG…I & II

By **Jelissa**

WHEN THE STREETS CLAP BACK I & II

By **Jibril Williams**

A DISTINGUISHED THUG STOLE MY HEART I II & III

By **Meesha**

PUSH IT TO THE LIMIT

By **Bre' Hayes**

BLOOD OF A BOSS **I, II, III & IV**

By **Askari**

THE STREETS BLEED MURDER **I, II & III**

THE HEART OF A GANGSTA I II& III

By **Jerry Jackson**

CUM FOR ME

CUM FOR ME 2

CUM FOR ME 3

An **LDP Erotica Collaboration**

BRIDE OF A HUSTLA **I II & II**

THE FETTI GIRLS **I, II& III**

CORRUPTED BY A GANGSTA

By **Destiny Skai**

WHEN A GOOD GIRL GOES BAD

By **Adrienne**

A GANGSTER'S REVENGE **I II III & IV**

THE BOSS MAN'S DAUGHTERS

THE BOSS MAN'S DAUGHTERS II

THE BOSSMAN'S DAUGHTERS III

THE BOSSMAN'S DAUGHTERS IV

A SAVAGE LOVE **I & II**

BAE BELONGS TO ME

A HUSTLER'S DECEIT I, II

By **Aryanna**

A KINGPIN'S AMBITON

A KINGPIN'S AMBITION **II**

I MURDER FOR THE DOUGH

By **Ambitious**

TRUE SAVAGE

TRUE SAVAGE II

TRUE SAVAGE **III**

TRUE SAVAGE **IV**

By **Chris Green**

A DOPEBOY'S PRAYER

By **Eddie "Wolf" Lee**

THE KING CARTEL **I, II & III**

By **Frank Gresham**

THESE NIGGAS AIN'T LOYAL **I, II & III**

By **Nikki Tee**

GANGSTA SHYT **I II &III**

By **CATO**

THE ULTIMATE BETRAYAL

By **Phoenix**

BOSS'N UP **I , II & III**

By **Royal Nicole**

I LOVE YOU TO DEATH

By Destiny J

I RIDE FOR MY HITTA

I STILL RIDE FOR MY HITTA

By **Misty Holt**

LOVE & CHASIN' PAPER

By **Qay Crockett**

TO DIE IN VAIN

By **ASAD**

BROOKLYN HUSTLAZ

By **Boogsy Morina**

BROOKLYN ON LOCK I & II

By **Sonovia**

GANGSTA CITY

By **Teddy Duke**

A DRUG KING AND HIS DIAMOND I & II

A DOPEMAN'S RICHES

By Nicole Goosby

TRAPHOUSE KING

By **Hood Rich**

LIPSTICK KILLAH **I, II**

By **Mimi**

BOOKS BY LDP'S CEO, CA$H

TRUST IN NO MAN

TRUST IN NO MAN 2

TRUST IN NO MAN 3

BONDED BY BLOOD

SHORTY GOT A THUG

THUGS CRY

THUGS CRY 2

THUGS CRY 3

TRUST NO BITCH

TRUST NO BITCH 2

TRUST NO BITCH 3

TIL MY CASKET DROPS

RESTRAINING ORDER

RESTRAINING ORDER 2

IN LOVE WITH A CONVICT

Coming Soon

BONDED BY BLOOD 2

BOW DOWN TO MY GANGSTA

LOVE SHOULDN'T HURT